RIVIERA REVENGE

GEORGE CAVENDISH

Order this book online at www.trafford.com
or email orders@trafford.com

Most Trafford titles are also available at major online book retailers.

Print information available on the last page.

ISBN: 978-1-4907-5942-5 (sc)
ISBN: 978-1-4907-5943-2 (e)

Library of Congress Control Number: 2015906685

Trafford rev. 10/23/2015

 www.trafford.com
North America & international
toll-free: 1 888 232 4444 (USA & Canada)
fax: 812 355 4082

Author Biographical Note

GEORGE CAVENDISH, son of a British army officer, spent his childhood in the Far East, notably India, Malaya and Hong Kong. Graduating from Oxford with a degree in Politics, Philosophy and Economics in 1974 he worked for 30 years in several international banks in Spain, Gibraltar, the City, France and Monaco. He lives on the French Riviera with his wife and children, now dedicating his time to reading, writing and various other fields of enjoyment and edification such as wine, opera and travel.

Contents

THIS BOOK FOLLOWS ON FROM *"RIVIERA TERMINUS"* which was set against the background of the Yugoslavian civil war. If you are one of the countless millions not to have read *"RT"* it will be necessary to at least have an idea of the story and main characters before embarking on *"Riviera Revenge"*, the latter being a sequel and therefore taking for granted that the reader is aware of who was whom and what happened before. In fact even if you have read *"RT"* a quick refresher might be useful! Please see the summary below.

RIVIERA TERMINUS

Summary

※

A SERBIAN WARLORD (**Vuk**) and his psychopathic partner (**Tomas**) leave the havoc of the civil war behind and arrive on the Côte d'Azur with a pile of dirty cash, some USD 16.000.000, earned from arms deals, prostitution and drugs. **Lucas**, a successful private banker (and lover of the good life) reckons he can help launder it (believing initially that it is "clean" money simply avoiding tax). But his hedonistic life lurches from pleasure to pain as Vuk becomes increasingly scary and the dubious origins of the money become known. Lucas struggles unsuccessfully to keep the deal under control and his drinking within limits.

While Lucas descends into an inferno of alcohol fuelled panic, an explosive cocktail of events also begins to conspire against Vuk: a young Bosnian Muslim (**Faruk**) based in Nice learns of his arrival and plans revenge for the murder of his family; Tomas betrays him and he (Vuk) falls in love with Faruk's beautiful sister (**Amra**) who wants to kill him.

But Vuk is tough and resourceful. It is touch and go to the end as to who survives and what happens to the money.

Somehow, Good triumphs over Evil and Vuk is killed by Amra in a dramatic finale on the "Grande Corniche" above Nice.

Lucas, his brother **George**, his assistant **Jérôme**, Amra and her brother Faruk share out Vuk's dirty loot between themselves, some three million USD each.

So we have a happy ending. But how happy can one be when the source of one's wealth is splattered in blood and when Vuk's fearsome twin brother, Krazicek, is alive and might come looking for revenge?

Finally, there is another USD three million sitting in a safe in Liechtenstein which Jérôme had deposited as part of the money laundering exercise. But it gets stolen by the Teubers, Lucas' wheeler-dealer banker/lawyer contacts in Liechtenstein. Should Lucas and his entourage stick their necks out again to try and get it back when they have so much already?

If it's just for the money then perhaps not. If it's a matter of principle then that's another matter!

Here's a bit more on the main characters:

Vuk Racik, wanted for crimes against humanity, is big, brutal, massively strong and highly intelligent. About 40 years old. He's a heavy drinker and a heavy consumer of prostitutes whom he likes to slap around. Needless to say he is totally unscrupulous, bordering on the sadistic.

Tomas, Vuk's sidekick, is apparently very loyal to Vuk but he becomes a traitor as he eyes the cash and wants a bigger share. Vuk disposes of him with a bullet in the head.

Lucas is a nice guy (a bit too complacent), English, 42 years old and manager of the Nice branch of a Swiss private bank. A "bon vivant", he loves women and drink and boosts his income with little deals on the side. But when he meets Vuk he gets out of his depth. He lives in the fast lane but is settling down with a young French girl, **Chloe**.

George, Lucas' younger brother, moves from London to the Riviera to join his brother and start a new life after a motorbike accident and an amorous deception. Good looking, straightforward and sensible he initially gets a job in a *brasserie* and lives in Lucas' apartment. He reluctantly gets dragged into the increasingly dangerous and frightening ramifications of the business deal between Vuk and Lucas. When he gets his share of the money at the end he is the only one to express misgivings, to himself, about the fact that it is dirty. One day he might just give it away!

Nathalie is a pretty (and very sexy) French girl whom George meets in the train on the way to Nice. She has a minor role in the story except at the end when we learn that she and George decide to shack up together......would George have preferred to stay with Amra with whom he has had an affair?

Jérôme, Lucas' trusted assistant at the bank, helps him with both normal banking business and their occasional private deals. Married with children, he is energetic and fun. He is essential to helping launder Vuk's money. While doing so, Tomas attempts to murder him but he survives.

Faruk is a young Bosnian Muslim who has managed to escape the Serbian maelstrom and settle on the Riviera. He has lost all his family (except his elder sister) to the Serbian paramilitaries. Faruk saw the murderers at the scene of the crime (amongst them Vuk) and has sworn revenge. He meets George by chance one day and they become friends. One day he recognizes Vuk, seated in the *brasserie* where he works.

Amra, Faruk's sister, works in Strasbourg but comes down to Nice when she hears her brother has, unbelievably, seen Vuk there. She comes initially to prevent Faruk acting rashly but when she finds him in hospital, paralyzed after an "accident", she assumes the role of avenger and decides to seduce Vuk (who of course has no idea who she is) and exact a terrible punishment. She and George are lovers until she decides to return to Bosnia to give humanitarian aid to her people.

Hans and Gerhardt Teuber, cousins, are banker and lawyer respectively, based in Liechtenstein, where they help Lucas and Jérôme launder the dirty cash. Gerhardt has a power of attorney on the account used to launder Vuk's money and the key to the safe where the cash gradually accumulates......

****

So *"Riviera Revenge"* picks up where *"Riviera Terminus"* left off, but nearly eight years later. The world has changed and another major geopolitical event is imminent, the 2003 invasion of Iraq. Inevitably it has a ripple effect across the world and forces the destiny of many of the above characters to crisscross in unexpected ways.

Of course the lives of Lucas, George, Amra, Jérôme and Faruk were linked already through their traumatic clash with Vuk Racik, and therefore indirectly to Vuk's twin brother Krazicek, although they had never met him. It was their teamwork which had resulted in the poetic justice of Vuk's "live by the sword die by the sword" *finale* on the *Grande Corniche* although it was Amra who actually executed him.

The build up to the Iraqi war ensures that their dormant relationship with Krazicek is activated. It sets the actors in motion, provoking intersections in their respective time and space which might not otherwise have occurred.

When 9/11 happened the dust was going to take a long time to settle, not just around the vestiges of the twin towers but right across the Middle East and in the heart of the offshore banking industry. Bush's invasion of Iraq shook things up in a big way.

It also had its impact, as we've mentioned above, on the lives of Krazicek and Lucas' entourage. They were all prompted, directly or indirectly, to leave their respective beaten tracks: Krazicek quickly realized he had to leave Baghdad; Lucas, fearful of the imminent avalanche of compliance and money laundering controls, was kick-started into trying to recoup the USD 3 million which had been stolen from the safe in Liechtenstein. ...... and a lot more.

It would not be long before they ended up breathing down each other's necks.

You should give so much of yourself to life and living that when the end comes there's nothing left for death to take". (I still haven't found out who the smart guy was who said that).

RIVIERA REVENGE

GERHARDT TEUBER

COSTA RICA combined just about everything a man could dream of. First were the two oceans; not many places on the planet where you could swim in the Pacific in the morning and in the Atlantic on the evening of the same day. A mere hundred miles (as the crow flies) separated the two oceans, but maybe eight hours driving along a mixture of passable motorway and rugged zig zagging bumpy tracks with no tarmac.

The country was ecologically protected, at least a third being classified national park, and the jungle to the south was dense, rich and a home to hundreds of varieties of wildlife. Further north were the mountains, the volcanoes, the lakes. On both sides endless sandy beaches with constant heavy waves picking up weight from a thousand miles away and making it a surfers' paradise.

And just about everywhere there were pretty girls anxious to make a living by providing a service to the generous tourists who came to surf, drink and fornicate.

There was no army in Costa Rica. There were very few money laundering controls. Foreigners fell into two categories: the wanted and the unwanted. Gerhardt was a bit of both, unwanted by anyone back home, hypothetically wanted by the international money laundering authorities had they known about him. Hans Teuber was on their list of suspects but Gerhardt had kept off the radar.

The extent and multiple sources of Gerhardt's fortune was impressive. Over the years of collaboration with his cousin Hans, he had amassed nearly thirty five million dollars, half of which he kept in a bank in Andorra and the other half divided between two banks in Costa Rica.

What Gerhardt Teuber loved most about his new life was the sense of control. Here he held his destiny in his own hands and nobody from his previous life in the drab Principality of Liechtenstein had the faintest idea as to his whereabouts. Apart from Hans of course, but years had gone by since he'd left and he and Hans had shared the spoils. Hans wasn't going to upset the apple cart. Even if he was a bit of a muttonhead.

Gerhardt Teuber started his usual morning routine. He pushed open the wooden door which led from his bedroom directly onto the tropical garden. His house stood a few hundred metres back from the Pacific Ocean.

First, a look at the flora. Three banana trees. That really made him happy for some reason, as if they symbolized the realisation of his dream. An impossible dream that had come true.

He wandered further down the path, which was bordered by a myriad of orchids and exotic cacti, and entered a small wooden cabin which was camouflaged beneath tangled ivy and fronted by magnificent clumps of pampas grass.

She was drying her hair. She smelled good and looked like an advertisement for sun cream. Her limbs were slim and strong, her tanned face glowing with youth. He paid her the equivalent of three hundred Euros a month. And of course she got food and shelter.

In return she cooked, cleaned and supplied Gerhardt with the weird sex he wanted.

This morning was no exception. He made her turn round, tied her hands behind her back and lifted her skirt. She grimaced as the painful humiliation began.

****

Gerhardt Teuber zipped up his shorts and walked back into the garden without a word. He walked slowly down to the beach, the rollers coming more and more into focus, beautiful, powerful and incessant.

He stripped off and had a short swim. He was not a good swimmer and was always intimidated by the force of the waves and the immediate sense of loneliness, as if he was the only person in the huge ocean. He completed some fifty metres of limp crawl and then left the foaming water. He walked, still nude, until the early morning sun had dried him off.

Costa Rica. Why the fuck did anyone go anywhere else?

WAKE UP CALL
2003

///

SOME SEVEN HOURS EARLIER and several thousand kilometres away, on the other side of the Atlantic, the same sun that was going to dry Gerhardt's body lit up the hills above Chateauneuf de Grasse and cast soft light on the roof of a villa belonging to the manager of Banque Helvas in Nice.

Lucas stared balefully into the mirror and did not like what he saw: his boyish good looks were barely discernible beneath the pallid, puffy skin of the face that greeted him. He turned sideways and tried unsuccessfully to hold in his paunch. Shit, he had let himself go in a big way. Gone were the halcyon days when he walked tall and proud and reeled in the female population of the Côte d'Azur with such facility.

He ran a comb through his hair and shaved. Then he put on his white bathrobe and rubbed his cheeks to inject a bit of colour. He peeped into the bedroom. Chloe was fast asleep as usual, doing her best to restore a modicum of energy to her tired body, build up at least some short term reserves to cope with the children. Not an easy time for her he reflected. Not an easy time for him. Chloe, suffering from post natal depression, had been on a love strike for nearly a year. His life was ticking by and he didn't want to go on pulling his wire on his own like a lonely adolescent.

He walked quietly and guiltily to the kitchen to get the coffee going. As the smell of the coffee reached his nostrils he looked around the room to find his cigarettes. He found them by the armchair next to an empty glass of wine. There was ash on the table. He looked back at the coffee machine, hesitated and left the cigarettes, picking up the glass to rinse it carefully in the sink.

How many years had gone by since it had all happened? Seven or eight? Whatever, the fact was he was fifty years old and feeling more like sixty. He poured out a large mug of coffee and sat down heavily to watch Sky News. That moron Bush with waggy tail Blair were really going to do it. They were going to invade Iraq, Bush playing out his John Wayne fantasy, Blair straining to camouflage his inadequacy and be a second Churchill.

Lucas felt the coffee warm him and wriggled his toes comfortably as he propped his feet on the table in front of his favourite armchair. Sky News droned on and he found his attention wandering to the bank.

Miraculously, he was still the manager. Miraculously, nobody outside the "famous five" as he had dubbed the inner circle, knew the truth about Vuk's demise and the money laundering that had preceded it.

But there were still a few things to sort out. The cash in the safe in Liechtenstein for example. Or, more precisely, sort out that Kraut bastard, Gerhardt Teuber, who had done a runner with the three million dollars that he was supposed to be holding in safe custody. It wasn't the lost money that infuriated Lucas so much as the fact that they had been cheated and taken for idiots. Why the hell had he waited so long?

Apathy. He'd had enough money already, more than enough and the money left over in the safe in Liechtenstein was like some kind of reserve. It could just sit there as far as he was concerned and be recouped at some later date. When he'd started getting a bit worried about it, particularly when the global money laundering psychosis flared up post 9/11, and had finally decided to empty the safety deposit box, it had been too late.

Hans Teuber, now retired from his post as manager of Baransteit Bank, swore his innocence and his ignorance of how and when his cousin Gerhardt had done the dirty deed. But Lucas wasn't sure he could believe him. Which meant he didn't believe him.

Lucas suddenly realized he wasn't in a fit state to do anything about it anyway. And that made him sit up. He put down his coffee cup and then stood up. He felt a small shot of adrenalin enter his bloodstream. He walked back to the bathroom, looked angrily at himself in the mirror again and whispered into his reflection.

"You're a lazy, useless, flatulent, alcoholic wreck Lucas. Hate yourself, punish yourself, kill yourself if you want to, what sodding difference is it going to make to the planet?"

He pulled off his pyjamas, winced as he saw his fat body in the harsh bathroom light and rummaged in a drawer under the basin. He found what he wanted. A pair of shorts and a heavy track suit top. Time to go in for repairs.

Two minutes later he was jogging heavily down the pathway leading to the country lane which fronted his house. He hoped no one was around to see his performance. Within a minute he was sweating. Within two minutes he was out of breath. After three minutes he slowed to a walk. He swung his arms around, punched the air and forced himself to start running again.

MONEY PROBLEMS

///

"SO YOU SEE? IT'S DIRTY MONEY SWEETHEART, not just dirty, filthy. It comes from drugs, prostitution, arms sales, you name it. We have to give it away. We have to give it back to the people who suffered most from its being generated in the first place."

George wound up his violent story about Vuk, the murders and the money laundering to a wide-eyed Nathalie. Why had he spent over seven years living with his misgivings and doing nothing about it?

Because he'd put it to the back of his mind, tucked the matter somewhere into a dark recess in his conscience while he lived the high life, spoilt Nathalie and enjoyed the feeling of having that enormous and secure cushion of cash.

And then things had changed. He'd started reading about what really happened during the Yugoslavian civil war, and it hit him like a sledgehammer that his fortuitous wealth was built on the proceeds of horrific suffering. Vuk's evil hands had collected the cash and were the same hands that had inflicted so much pain and death. When Amra had pumped all those bullets into Vuk, the bullets he so deserved, he and the others had scooped up the cash like so many birds of prey, without a second thought about its diabolical origins.

Now he had to release the demons buzzing around in his head and the only way to do that was speak to someone close. Who better than Nathalie?

He waited expectantly for her reaction.

Nathalie looked at him with silent amazement. So this was what George had got mixed up with. This was the background to his apparent wealth which she had always found so strange. He'd even played quite an important role. He'd steered Amra to the Bosnian cell in Nice and he'd physically transported her to the Grande Corniche where she had executed Vuk. But he'd shown naivety too. And he was showing even greater naivety now, wanting to give away millions of dollars.

"George," she said carefully. "This money belongs to us, I mean to you..... you know what I mean. This money came to us, to you, providentially. You can't just give it away. We have a right to be happy too. It would be irresponsible to give it away. How would you know if the persons you gave it to used it properly? How would you even know whom to give it to? Even charities are corrupt. George, please don't be stupid, don't be naïve. *Zut alors!*"

George felt a sting of anger. He hadn't expected her to be so hard headed, to fall so short of the empathy and understanding he had been so sure of receiving. He felt the trickle of disappointment seep into his bloodstream.

"Nath, you're my partner, my friend, my lover. Surely you can understand my misgivings, why I need to clean this whole thing out of my system. I'm losing sleep Nath, I wake up having nightmares, about innocent citizens being shot by terrorists armed with machine guns supplied by Vuk Racik. I think of those poor girls from Eastern Europe who are bullied into prostitution, the junkies.......That money is so tainted even a vulture wouldn't want it. It's got to go Nath."

Nathalie lowered her eyes and felt her heart harden. She had only sought a quick fling with George when she had met him, seven years ago, on the train. She'd found him so attractive. But when she had come down to Nice with the intention of spending a couple of weeks (mainly in bed) with him she had not anticipated the apparently unlimited supply of money he was prepared to spend.

And so she had stayed. She was twenty eight years old now. All options were open. She was young, beautiful and sharp as a razor. She flicked her thick chestnut hair off her forehead and spoke quietly.

"Just let me think about it a bit more George. Please don't do anything for the moment."

******

Nearly eight years. That was a long chapter by any standards and although Nathalie did not feel pressed by time she needed to take stock and evaluate her relationship with George.

George was perfect in a way. In many ways. Maybe that was part of the problem. Handsome, gentle, generous, virile....but something was missing and she thought she had nearly identified what it was. For all his qualities and charm he seemed nevertheless to be absent sometimes, albeit imperceptibly.

His kindness was genuine but lacked total spontaneity and he was not as amusing as when they had first met. Maybe this was the way it went, the way of all emotions, a gradual wearing down of the surface of their love with the fine sandpaper of time and routine. But she thought it went beyond that, as if some quiet melancholy was seeping into his mind. If she hadn't been totally convinced of his fidelity she would have automatically suspected the presence of another woman in his life. But there wasn't another woman, she knew that.

And then she had to acknowledge that her own feelings did not bear close scrutiny. Indifference was surreptitiously gaining ground in her heart and the clammy hand of boredom was clutching at her life. How was it possible when they made such a perfect couple?

It was possible because she no longer felt passion when she made love; it was possible because she found it more and more difficult to maintain that effervescent dialogue which had characterised their first few years; it was possible because George and she simply didn't quite function on the same wavelength.

It was possible she had fallen out of love. It was certain that she felt restless.

George's quaint misgivings about the money were not going to help restore an amorous equilibrium.

23

THE TWIN
2003

WHEN KRAZICEK WAS ABOUT to enter his hotel room he realized someone had preceded him and it wasn't the time of day for the cleaning lady. The tiny film of powder he left on the door handle had gone. The question was whether he or she, or they, were there to kill him or just to spy. Whoever had entered was certainly still there because he had only been absent ten minutes. He would soon find out.

He had a simple contingency plan which as far as he knew nobody else had used: a tear gas grenade attached behind the main lamp above his bed could be detonated from a remote control which he carried on his key ring. The wall cavity outside his room, which lodged a fuse box and a large red fire hydrant, also hid a gas mask.

His pulse barely changed as he activated the grenade and put on the mask. He could hear the mild explosion and the hiss of the gas. He waited five seconds and burst into his room. Two men were gasping and swearing as they staggered blindly, crashing into each other and falling over bits of furniture.

Krazicek landed one sledgehammer blow on the back of the head of the closest intruder and a lethal kick in the other's groin. He knew the first would be unconscious for half an hour. If he wasn't already in a coma. The other wouldn't be able to talk for five minutes.

He opened the French windows which led to the balcony and switched on a fan. The air cleared rapidly but there was going to be a lingering acrid stench. He took off his mask carefully and sniffed the air. It was breathable.

He looked down at the bodies on the floor, one inert and strangely peaceful despite the blood oozing out of both ears, the other pale as a fish belly, conscious and only able to breathe with short painful gasps as his hands vainly covered his testicles.

"That looks painful," said Krazicek. "I'll give you one more minute and then you tell me who you are and what the fuck you want....what you wanted."

The man looked quite big, although it was difficult to judge when he was sprawled on the floor. Maybe six feet two, ninety five kilos. Krazicek had three inches and twenty kilos advantage. Twenty kilos of healthy and unusually strong muscle.

He looked at his watch and then patted the stricken man's pockets from which he extracted a slim revolver.

"Shit. You intending to use this on me?"

The man shook his head, still horribly pale and shocked.

"You working for Sadaam, one of the arms dealers or the CIA?"

The man remained silent, looking confused and scared. Krazicek squatted down by him and placed the revolver in the man's right hand and forced him to point it directly at his companion's head. He started to squeeze the trigger.

"CIA."

"You stupid nosey bastards." He grabbed the man's hair and pulled his neck back to breaking point. "Looking for something to incriminate me? What did you think, that you were going to find a stash of Kalashnikovs?"

The wounded man stared at Krazicek with surrender in his eyes. He reminded Krazicek of a deer lying in the road after an encounter with a heavy goods vehicle.

"OK Bambi, what do I do with you? Shoot you now or give you a chance?"

Bambi's eyes changed expression. "What can I do?" He asked feebly.

"You phone whomever sent you here and tell them you got here too late, the bird has flown, the room is empty, there are no incriminating documents. You got nothing. Say that reception informs you that Krazicek Racik left for Hong Kong three days ago."

Bambi did as he was told. As soon as he had finished he received, in return, a powerful blow to the jaw. It snapped like a dry twig. He bound both men together and wrapped thick sticky tape round their mouths.

Krazicek dusted off his trousers and walked out of the French windows and contemplated the busy streets of Baghdad from his balcony at the top of the Hilton Hotel.

What a dump. Years of his life in Iraq. He'd made good money, that was for sure, but he could never adapt to the place. This was not his culture, the people were not his people and living in a Muslim country for a Serb did not exactly induce inner peace and harmony. And now the fucking CIA was breathing down his neck.

He looked at the Sunday Herald report which he had left on the balcony table and rapidly concluded that the time had come to move on to pastures new. Pastures like the South of France where his beloved Vuk, his twin brother, had got murdered. If he found out who was really responsible for that he was going to plan a very painful revenge. Why the fuck had he waited so long before hunting down the killers?

Money. He was earning so much and he didn't want to fall off his perch at the top of the arms trafficking trade between Yugoslavia and Iraq. Any absence for more than a few weeks would have been fatal. It was a dirty business and those involved played dirty tricks.

He flicked his cigarette over the balcony and watched it whirl hopelessly down to the street, occasionally bumping against the building's facade. Rather like someone being pushed out of a window he thought.

He started reading the article in the Sunday Herald again:

A new report finds the Yugoslavian government has helped Sadaam Hussein build up a terrifying arsenal.

High-level military and civilian officials of the Former Republic of Yugoslavia (FRY) have clearly known about, and therefore been implicitly involved in, a massive arms-for-cash trade with Iraq that has continued in the last two years, in violation of international agreements and explicit promises to

American and European authorities. The assistance to Iraq, illegal under UN sanctions imposed in 1990, could end up being used against allied forces should military action be launched against Iraq.

Despite his cynicism, Krazicek felt a current of pride sweep through his mind. Sure, massive arms-for-cash deals which he had brokered! That was why he was so rich. The fact that the arms would be used to kill people didn't quite get to him. There was too much money at stake and the stupid bastards would kill each other anyway, with or without his help. And so he swept the matter underneath the carpet of his conscience. Not that the latter had ever been particularly sensitive.

The extent of this Yugo-Iraqi axis is the subject of a detailed report, "Arming Saddam" from the non-profit international research and advocacy organisation, The International Crisis Group (ICG).

The ICG report makes clear the illicit Yugoslav arms trade with Iraq is not the result of unauthorised, 'rogue' operations, as previously claimed by FRY leaders, but a steady pipeline that has generated hundreds of millions, perhaps billions, of dollars for state-run and private companies with ties to political parties and military and civilian leaders - monies believed to have largely migrated to illegal offshore bank accounts.

Krazicek frowned. Shit, better check things out with the bank in Switzerland. Maybe set up new arrangements. He didn't want the CIA sniffing around. One thing was a couple of agents visiting his hotel room. Another would be a methodical search for his burgeoning bank account. Bastards.

The report concludes that despite recent statements of disavowal from top officials, including the Yugoslav president and

Serbian premier, internal documents indicate they must have had prior knowledge of the Iraqi trade.

ICG cites high-level sources in the Democratic Opposition of Serbia, the ruling government coalition, as affirming that the deliberately mislabelled cargoes were escorted to the Montenegrin ports of Bar and Tivat by the Serbian, Montenegrin and Yugoslav federal interior ministries.

Yugoslavia appears to have sold Iraq anti-aircraft systems, artillery, munitions, and constructed underground bunker complexes inside Iraq. The combination of technologies provided by Yugoslavia could enable the Iraqi government to create an inexpensive cruise missile with weapons of mass destruction.

A number of key figures control a web of trading companies implicated in the arms traffic, backed by a consortium of financiers pulling the strings in "respectable" institutions including Swiss and other offshore centres ensuring it is nearly impossible to track the ultimate recipients of the profits.

Krazicek made a small sigh of relief.

The network of corruption is alarming: it makes a mockery of existing systems of prevention, control and protection which are infiltrated by the very perpetrators of the crimes they are supposed to prevent.

"Tough," he said out loud. He felt strong, he felt invulnerable.

BACK IN THE BANK

///

JÉRÔME SAT IN HIS OFFICE, sipping his coffee and waiting for Lucas. Both men were trying to work out a strategy for recouping the three million Dollars which Gerhardt Teuber had stolen from the safe in Barantsteitbank. The matter had become more urgent all of a sudden with the current, and growing, political phobia about money laundering. If they were to get the money back and somehow filter it into legitimate bank accounts in their own names they had to move quickly.

A whole new tidal wave of controls and legislation was expected now that the invasion of Iraq was a virtual certainty and the authorities were working themselves into a frenzy over its alleged links to Al Qaeda and their shared mechanisms for financing the acquisition of arms.

Why had he not done anything about it before? Because Jérôme was satisfied with what he had and didn't really want to embark on any strategy at all. He had escaped an untimely death at the hands of the psychopathic Tomas, was now worth over three million dollars himself and led a tranquil existence on the Côte d'Azur. He was forty two years old and his children were growing up nicely.

"*Tout baigne huh?*"* said Lucas, suddenly appearing at the door of Jérôme's office.

Jérome smiled and followed Lucas through to his office. Their morning routine. Lucas' office remained something of a haven, comfortable, spacious and tasteful. It had changed in the fifteen years it had been occupied by him: the light blue of the walls had been replaced by white and the grey carpet by teak parquet but the expensive and still modern looking furniture and generously sized mahogany desk remained the same. His drinks cabinet in particular sported the same whiskies, crystal decanter and glasses.

---

* "*Everything OK?*"

"*Tout baigne?* Yes, I think so, I seem to be growing older quite peacefully."

"Growing older is an issue of mind over matter Jérôme."

"How so Lucas?"

"If you don't mind it doesn't matter."

"I'll try not to laugh too much *Patron*. Only wine is supposed to improve with time but I'm not complaining. Happy to cruise along, you know."

"Things never stay the same in life," said Lucas. "You should know that by now, especially after what you've been through. Don't get complacent. The real cancer of time is complacency. If there is something you want to do, or should do, you'd better pull your finger out. One life Jérôme."

Jérome smiled again.

"You're looking slightly different this morning," remarked Jérôme.

"More handsome and intelligent?"

"Impossible. But, well, sort of .....different."

"Remember what you said about wine Jérôme. You can compare me to a good Bordeaux. I get better as the years go by. Smoother, deeper, more velvety....."

"Rounder?" interrupted Jérôme.

Lucas' propensity to put on weight had been accentuated by his playing less tennis and his insatiable appetite for wine. His cellar at home had been filling up by the day, marginally faster than he was emptying it.

"I've started working out Jérôme."

"When?"

"Three days ago."

They both laughed.

"You wait," said Lucas. "One kilo a week is the target. Morning jog, Krav Maga classes in the evening and no alcohol."

"Krav Maga?"

"Yup, Krav Maga, that way I'm going to be able to rip off Gerhardt Teuber's bollocks and break his neck all in one go. He stole three million dollars from us. Remember that? Why let him get away with it?"

"We've got to find him first. He could be anywhere. The world's a big place."

"South America, I'm sure, that's where all these Krauts go."

Jérôme adopted his nice adult talking to backward child voice. "South America is smaller than the world but it's still big."

Lucas ignored him and poured himself some coffee. "I want to get that fat bastard and South America is the best place to start looking for him."

"Sure Lucas, good thinking."

Lucas sat down again. "Jérôme, just how close do you think Gerhardt and Hans Teuber were......are?"

"Difficult to say with the *Allemands*. They are not quite the same as us. A bit stunted on the emotional side. But put it this way, they were close enough in my view to hatch a plot together, cover each others' arses and steal our money from the safe."

"Which means two things, if you're right. Firstly it means Hans Teuber knows where Gerhardt is."

"Agreed," said Jérôme. "We've always suspected that but never been able to prove it and Hans has never given in to our questioning."

Lucas stood up yet again and started talking more intensely. "The second thing is that we are not the only victims."

"What do you mean?"

"Think about it. Hans Teuber, manager of Baransteitbank Liechtenstein for fifteen years doesn't just meet one client putting cash and valuables into a safety deposit box. He meets dozens of them and many require a local attorney empowered to sign on the account and even keep the key to the safe, just like us. As time goes by, some of the beneficial owners die, some get dementia and forget and some get murdered. I wonder how many safes, how many accounts were controlled by Gerhardt Teuber? And there's no way he operated without the help of cousin Hans. They must have tens of millions stashed away."

Jérôme nodded his head thoughtfully. "You have become French Lucas. You combine Cartesian logic with a suspicious mind and always assume the worst about human nature."

"Please, anything but French, you know my opinions."

Jérôme did indeed know his 'opinions': according to Lucas the French suffered from some kind of existential gloom inculcated from nursery school onwards. Their educational system and cultural mentality made them unhappy when in fact, if one combined their standard of living, generous welfare and health systems, the natural richness and diversity of their country, gastronomic traditions and unlimited good wine, they should be among the happiest people on earth.

"Are you aware?" He would ask Jérôme, "that France has the highest suicide rate in Europe? Suicide is the biggest cause of mortality after road accidents! It's something in your culture which makes you poor bastards miserable. Plus the fact that you never have a proper breakfast. You fuck your liver with thick black coffee and croissants dripping with grease and that puts you in a bolshy mood for the rest of the day. You never say *'Oui'*, you always say *'Oui mais'*, you drive like homicidal maniacs to compensate for your sense of inadequacy, you're rude, hypocondriachal and trapped in a useless intellectual format which provokes endless sterile debate but never any practical conclusion."

Jérôme, preparing for a good natured rant from his *'patron'*, was wont to goad him on at this stage and allude to 'anachronistic British colonial arrogance' and jealousy over France's glorious history and culture.

"French history my friend", Lucas would shoot back, "consists of Charlemagne (who goes back to the dark ages and is therefore no longer of relevance), Louis XV (*'Après moi le déluge'* and sure enough, metaphorically speaking, it's never stopped raining since he died), *'La Révolution'* (a bloodbath with old hags sitting around knitting as they watched the flower of the French Aristocracy being guillotined, including their last king, Louis XVI) and

Napoleon (a Corsican megalomaniac with a small prick who decided to conquer the world to prove he had a big one).

"And Napoleon was the last person to really influence the way France is run: the legal system, the educational system and the political philosophy and infrastructure in this country all derive from this neurotic dwarf who designed them two hundred years ago!"

"What about Charles de Gaulle?"

"Oh sorry," Lucas would reply, "You mean that bloke who ran away when the Germans invaded but somehow convinced France that it was he who won the war?"

Jérôme enjoyed Lucas' sardonic caricatures because they served a purpose; they kept alive an interesting debate and underscored Lucas' ambivalence as a francophile Englishman living in France who nevertheless compulsively poured out francophobe utterances as a way of asserting that he had not forsaken his cultural roots. But even if Lucas was supposed to be joking it was interesting how cruelly barbed his jokes really were when compared to the somewhat indulgent, humorous and gentle mockery of the French about the English. Why were the British so virulent in their dislike and suspicion of the French?

At the same time it was true that behind every caricature was an element of truth. French despondency manifested itself in multi-faceted dissatisfaction and depressiveness, lack of trust, cynicism about other people and an attitude problem.

A contradictory backdrop of nostalgia over lost colonial grandeur juxtaposed with anti-capitalism, an elitist school system disguised as egalitarian, fervent belief in *"La liberté"* while favouring a pervasive and strong government and a sinking feeling that the French language itself was being ineluctably suppressed by the universal adoption of English, did not help. All of it translated into an exceptionally high consumption of psychoactive drugs.

"Anyway," continued Lucas intensely, "if we managed to find Gerhardt we wouldn't just find our three million dollars, we'd find more, a lot more, and that opens up a whole new dimension."

Jérôme watched Lucas pacing up and down.

"Oh shit," he said. "You know something? This reminds me of when you first discussed Vuk Racik and his sixteen million dollars. You were all pepped up like this and we nearly all got killed. Me in particular."

"A whole new dimension Jérôme," Lucas muttered again under his breath. "I'm going to find you Gerhardt Teuber, just you wait....." He broke into a barely recognizable parody of Eliza Doolittle, "I'll have your head Gerhardt Teuber...."

Jérôme winced, Lucas' tuneless rendition leaving him with no desire to discover the rest of *My Fair Lady*.

"Il commence à pleuvoir Lucas."

---

* *"It's started raining Lucas" (French expression: when somebody sings out of tune it brings on the rain)*

BROTHERS

///

"SO THIS CHAP GOES INTO A DOCTOR'S SURGERY," said Lucas.

George braced himself. Was this going to be good, bad or indifferent?

"And he says to the receptionist, 'I want to see the doctor.' The receptionist asks him for his name and he replies 'Smith'.

"'Well Mr Smith, may I ask what you want to consult the doctor about?'

"And the chap says 'My cock.'"

George felt a flicker of amusement.

"So there's this uncomfortable stirring amongst the other patients in the waiting room, you know, slight rustling of newspapers, and the receptionist says:

'Really Mr Smith, I must ask you to express yourself more discreetly, you are embarrassing everybody.'

"Smith scratches his head and replies 'OK, I want to see the doctor about my ear.'

"'That's better, thank you Mr Smith. And what is the problem with your ear?'

"'I can't piss out of it.'"

Lucas accompanied the punch line with a hoot of laughter.

George relaxed and looked around Lucas' wine cellar with admiration.

"So, just like old times."

The two brothers sat together, George sipping rosé and Lucas mineral water. Two months had gone by since Lucas' conversion to a healthy lifestyle. Two months of iron discipline which had already made him look ten years younger. And ten kilos lighter.

"Yeah," said Lucas.

There was a moment's silence.

"Want to listen to a bit more about my plans?" Lucas asked.

"What worries me about your plans Lucas, what I've gathered so far anyway, is that they basically involve trying to get more dirty money and probably putting your life at risk again. Not to mention mine. And others'."

"Don't be such a drama queen. You're all tensed up, you should do some yoga. Listen, we all got rich thanks to me. Now we can get richer. Do you want in or not?"

George looked at his brother with his habitual mixture of incredulity and admiration. "So you want to get richer?"

"No, all I want is the chance to prove to myself that having more money won't make me happier."

"Seriously, there are other things in life."

"For example?"

"Er...love?"

"I agree George, money is not the most important thing in the world. Love is. And I love money."

"Why be so clever and cynical Lucas? In the long run you become a victim of your wealth and you adjust your life to your money. It preoccupies your thoughts and creates all these artificial needs...it just draws a curtain between you and the real world."

"Frankly," replied Lucas, "who needs the real world? Anyway, first of all I want you to try this." He got up and walked over to his Grand Cru rack of Bordeaux and reached for one of his best bottles, Château la Tour 1987.

He placed it on the improvised table, an upturned barrel, opened it carefully and started decanting it

"This should be divine."

George observed him. He wasn't going to question Lucas about his apparently impromptu decision to climb off the wagon.

"Tell me something Lucas. Has it ever occurred to you that the word 'divine' might mean of the vine?"

"Haven't got a clue. But I like the idea." Lucas finished decanting the wine and half filled two glasses.

"You know one of the few things I like about you Lucas?"

"No."

"You have this amazing collection of wine but you never talk about it. You're not one of those wine bores going on about vintages and texture and colour and all the other stuff. You just drink it."

They sipped and grunted appreciatively. Lucas swirled his wine around in the glass and studied it against the light. He recited:

« *Wine comes in at the mouth*
And love comes in at the eye;
That's all we shall know for truth
Before we grow old and die."

"Good wine has got soul," he continued. "It's the one which should do the talking, not me. It's like meeting someone who impresses you, someone who has a quality which crosses a boundary in your mind and you want to listen and learn from him. Something to do with life force. When you feel it you're kind of grateful because you realize you shouldn't have allowed yourself to grow deaf to certain things. Refined things. It puts you back in touch with what you thought was intangible."

George nodded. "I guess I know what you mean."

"Of course you do, you're my brother. Soul is the truest most profound part, the thing you can't change. Not to be confused with personality, which is cosmetic and superficial, the outward appearance which cloaks the inner essence. Very modern tendency that by the way. The best way to overlook the soul of a wine is to break it down into its parts and talk about that stuff you mentioned, colour, tannic quality, body..... I hate it, style over substance."

George stood up and studied the rack of Grand Cru, gently extracting a dusty bottle of *Pomerol*.

"So how do you describe the soul of this Lucas?"

"Pulchritudinous," replied Lucas seriously.

"Fucking hell. And what about this, *Margaux* .....?"

"Magnanimous."

"Amazing. And this, *St Emilion*?"

"Sanctimonious."

"Nice, they all alliterate. And I suppose your *Cheval Blanc* is chivalrous? I knew you were taking the piss."

"I'm not actually. Anyway, this is how things get going George. First you open a good bottle, then you drink it and then, once sufficiently mellowed, you look at things in an uninhibited and positive manner and decide to act."

"That is about the most facile bit of reasoning I have ever heard," replied George. "You don't just opt for action as if you're going to a fun fair for God's sake. You don't just extract a plan out of a wine bottle. Ever heard of logic and strategy?"

Lucas smiled at his younger brother. "I didn't know you'd attended Harvard business school."

"Common sense Lucas. Nothing fancy."

Lucas took another sip and looked George in the eyes.

"I want to hunt down that Gerhardt bastard. In fact I want to hunt down every bastard I can find before I die. The world is populated by greedy, vicious bastards."

George stared aghast. "What the fuck is eating you? Hey Lucas, you're not turning into some kind of fundamentalist are you? What is all this crusading crap? Go back to drinking and womanising for God's sake, it suits you better."

"I'm being serious. The world is imploding. Corrupt politicians, dishonest bankers, unscrupulous multinationals, drug pedlars, Serbian warlords, arms dealers, Osama Bin Laden, Mugabe, Gerhardt Teuber....."

"You've lost it."

"I know. Up to a point. But I feel angry. I feel rebellious. I need to hit out. Gerhardt is just the first obvious target. He's treated us like idiots. We're all just lying back like pigs in shit. It's not about the money George. Sod the money. The world's a foul place and yet most people are actually nice so it must be the minority bastards who are making it all go wrong. It's as if the power of evil is stronger than the power of good. And that's because the good guys are mostly apathetic and just want to get on with their lives quietly, you know, keep out of trouble, go with the flow....."

"Dead fish go with the flow," said George and then sat back. He realized Lucas was echoing his own subconscious thoughts, ones which he had never voiced. This was not the Lucas he thought he knew, this was a new version.

"You know something?"

"What?" asked Lucas.

"I actually understand what you are saying. I feel the same. I just can't believe I'm hearing this from you. I feel deeply angry too, indignant, call it what you like, all those manipulative bastards out there taking the piss out of us, out of everybody. Giving away my money is a sop to my conscience. And my conscience can't be that strong because I've managed to hang on to the money for the last seven years. What I really fantasize about is killing off the Vuks of this world, punishing the Hans' and Gerhardts. Crazy stuff."

Lucas laughed. "If you're thinking like that we could make a good team."

They looked at each other in silence for a few seconds. A new fraternal bond.

"You still haven't answered my question Lucas."

"What question ?"

"What the fuck does 'in' mean?"

"I've got a plan. We'll talk about it tomorrow with Jérôme. Tonight we're going to talk about Nathalie."

He had to tell George that he thought Nathalie was behaving strangely. In fact he had always found Nathalie a bit strange. He had never really liked her. How to broach the subject with George, that was the difficult bit. He poured out the remainder of the wine.

LETTER FROM VUK
JULY 1995

///

KRAZI,

How are things? Long time no see but as soon as I get my stuff sorted we'll meet. Somewhere nice.

You know something? We've done well. You must be up to thirty million by now, banked and safe. I've got the original funds I left on your Swiss account (five million with interest) and sixteen million cash from when I got out of Yugoslavia, although it's not all banked.

Anyway, you stick to Baghdad for the moment and I'll stay here in Nice until the banking shit is finished and then we'll have one hell of a party!

I've found a banker to look after the cash. Clever guy, English, but he's weak and scared of me so I don't expect any problems. He's got this French assistant called Jérôme whose doing the real job getting the cash to Liechtenstein and he's OK. I think he's OK, you never know!

The girls are quite good down here. Same as everywhere I guess. Tomas and I are thinking of setting up our own business, getting some of the bitches over from Serbia, maybe even some of the bitches from Bosnia. Much cheaper, big margins, easy to control. When you wind up your business with Saddam and his cronies and the heat is off you should come and join us. Keep yourself busy.

For the moment no 'phone calls, in fact I'm not even going to give you my number. You're in the clear, everyone thinks we're estranged after that so called fight we had in Zagreb! That was a clever move although you nearly broke my nose you bastard. I liked the way you denounced me as a traitor when I disappeared from Yugoslavia! Why are we so much cleverer than those Milosevic sycophants? Or are they just stupid?

When all is clear I'll let you know, same channels, and we'll fix where to meet.

Stay cool

Vuk

The "channels" were very simple. Vuk had established contact with a local French company in Saint Laurent du Var exporting medical equipment to Iraq which was allowed in on humanitarian grounds and avoided the trade embargo. The equipment included syringes, antiseptic, bandages and a variety of antibiotics. When he wanted to write to his brother he slipped a couple of five hundred Franc notes to one of the employees in the packaging department who tucked his letter into a box addressed to the Red Cross mission in Baghdad. Krazicek looked after the rest at his end.

Extreme precautions, but these were extreme times. It was a paradox really. The CIA's telecommunications surveillance systems had become so sophisticated that it was dangerous even to use an anonymous mobile telephone. Krazicek was under surveillance by definition so any call, however coded or disguised would be followed up and Vuk would be tracked down. Hence the resort to old-fashioned tactics which were laughable by modern standards. But efficient.

Krazicek sent messages back to "poste restante" at the main Nice post office for the attention of Josef Havel, his brother's new identity after he'd left Serbia.

Then he had heard of Vuk's death.

Krazicek read the letter a last time. He'd kept it for nearly eight years. He took out his pocket lighter and watched it burn. He felt guilty.

Then he reflected on the background to his fortune and his future:

In 1990 Yugoslavia was among a small group of poorer countries with industrial economies actively developing arms export industries. The country sold almost two billion dollars worth of weapons to Iraq in its war with Iran during the eighties, a mere fraction of what was sold, both to Iraq and other countries, in the nineties.

The Middle East and North Africa were the prime markets. Many top customer countries were members of the Nonaligned Movement. Among other weapons and equipment, Yugoslavia exported ammunition, antiarmor and antitank weapons systems, frigates, missile boats, Mala swimmer delivery vehicles, the Orao ground attack fighter and the Partisan helicopter. Krazicek climbed on board the arms gravy train in the early nineties.

Iraq proved to be a huge market and anyone unscrupulous enough to broker the arms deals (or lucky enough, depending on one's point of view) could skim off a vast amount of money from both suppliers and end users and indeed a myriad of intermediaries. Krazicek worked this out for himself when he saw what Vuk was earning by selling arms to Libya. He also worked out how the offshore banking system could help him hide his ill gotten gains.

He remembered watching the movie, *The Third Man*, and Orson Welles' memorable soliloquy: "In Italy, for thirty years under the Borgias, they had warfare, terror, murder and bloodshed, but they produced Michelangelo, Leonardo da Vinci, and the Renaissance. In Switzerland, they had brotherly love, five hundred years of democracy and peace, and what did they produce? The cuckoo clock."

Krazicek could never quite understand those lines. The Swiss had produced much more than cuckoo clocks. They had also produced the world's most sophisticated banking industry which, *inter alia*, oiled the wheels of the arms trade between Iraq and Yugoslavia (not to mention Nazi imports of commodities during the war, the global drugs trade and the illegal transfer of funds from a variety of banana republics to credit the savings accounts of their respective dictators).

When UN sanctions were imposed on Yugoslavia in May 1992 because of the Bosnia war, Milosevic, the leader of Serbia at the time, had already anticipated the embargo and established the infrastructure for exploiting the international banking and trading systems to bust sanctions and keep exporting arms and importing vital commodities. Krazicek's fortune grew in tandem.

The elaborate operation was centred on Cyprus because of its banking secrecy, offshore companies culture, and the sympathy of Greek Cypriots for the plight of their fellow Orthodox Serbs. Cyprus was the conduit for billions of dollars in cash from Serbia. The funds were then dispersed globally or into the accounts of scores of anonymously owned offshore companies, including Fairtrade Corporation which belonged to Krazicek.

Fantastic sums of money were generated by arms sales to Iraq. Analysis of Sadaam Hussein's secret money-laundering techniques showed how he used the same offshore money launderers as Osama bin Laden. That covert money network, based in the tax havens of Switzerland, Liechtenstein, Panama and Nassau, helped bankroll the war machines of both Iraq and al-Qaeda. Krazicek found that of academic interest, no more.

Sadaam had begun constructing his offshore operation in 1968 in Switzerland, aware that the country's bank secrecy made it a prime place to organize the movement of illicit funds and the purchase of arms. He constructed a network to launder secret commissions charged on sales of Iraqi crude oil. The system also would be used for kickbacks on purchases from Western arms dealers. Liechtenstein was used to ensure even more impenetrable secrecy: real names of company and account owners would be hidden from law enforcers.

Paper shell companies in New York City, London, Paris, Milan, Vienna, Tokyo, Seoul and Sao Paolo had shares of other companies that carried out the money laundering and arms purchases.

The totals from skimmed oil revenues and contract kickbacks from the late 1970s through the oil-for-food nineties and the build up to the 2003 invasion of Iraq had been estimated by U.S. officials to reach thirty or forty billion dollars. What amazed Krazicek was how easy it had been to get a slice of it.

In the hunt for Sadaam Hussein's billions, investigators had identified five networks, of more than a hundred companies each, used to launder money skimmed from Iraqi oil sales and arms purchases. Krazicek used the sixth network, which they couldn't find. A network which brought together arms trading with Iraq and narcotics and terrorism in Afghanistan. The investigators knew it had to exist but it was like trying to catch a ghost, a slippery one at that. Krazicek's commissions were channelled through the labyrinthine sixth network to Fairtrade Corporation which had its account with UNSB in Geneva.

His fortune had grown immeasurably as he continued to broker the vast deals with the Sadaam regime but his anger and pain had not subsided.

He flicked his mind back to Vuk.

Eight years was a long time. He asked himself the same question again: why hadn't he tried to track down his brother's killers before? Because he'd been too busy making money. Maybe also because underneath he knew that Vuk lived so dangerously that it was inevitable that one day he be the one on the wrong end of a bullet. Vuk had done some pretty rough stuff. Whatever, the time had come to seek revenge and the clues in Vuk's letter were as good a way as any for him to make a start.

He was glad to be on the move, and the sight of the two CIA agents on the floor, whom he couldn't quite bring himself to kill in cold blood, made him even gladder. There would be many more from where they came from. Another good reason to leave.

He looked over his luxury hotel room, where he had lived for eight years, without sentiment or nostalgia. He was going to fly to Madrid, stay a few days, or weeks if necessary, and then to Nice via Dubai on a different passport. He decided to call Peletier, his relationship manager in UNSB in Geneva, when he arrived in Nice rather than straight away. No point in raising suspicion by calling too soon after the publication of the Sunday Herald report.

He checked his luggage and counted his money. He had emptied his Baghdad bank account that afternoon. He had two hundred and fifty thousand dollars in cash and of course his credit cards drawn on his Panama registered company, Fairtrade Ltd. But he didn't like using them, they left a trail and were reserved for emergencies. A further one and a half million Euros were readily available in Banco Santander in Madrid. Another two million dollars in a bank in Panama. He had more than enough to get by on for the moment. No need to disturb his core savings in UNSB, a princely eighty five million dollars.

He carried his two suitcases to the lifts and descended to the hotel foyer.

"I want nobody in my room, no cleaning lady, nobody, until tomorrow." Krazicek placed fifty dollars on the counter.

The hotel staff knew better than to question instructions from their best and most generous client.

"That is understood Sir, nobody will enter your room until tomorrow."

"Good."

The bill, which he paid every month, had been settled and he walked outside into the heat. Within seconds a taxi pulled up, summoned by one of the doormen, and Krazicek, having climbed in and instructed the driver to take him to the airport, stared out at the dusty urban landscape for a last time.

SEYCHELLES

JÉRÔME PICKED UP THE TELEPHONE and called his "Corporate Services Provider", a one man band in Cyprus who knew exactly where to go and how to activate an off the shelf company anywhere in the world. His favourite location at the moment, "flavour of the month" as he put it, was the Seychelles. He also acted as a business introducer to a number of banks in various offshore centres and could ensure the opening of a bank account within forty eight hours.

"Two companies then, nominee directors and shareholders, use your usual trust arrangements to keep us at a distance. The signatories on the bank accounts should be corporate, that is to say whichever company represents the trust. And they take instructions from any of the three beneficial owners: me, Lucas and George Watt. Special fee arrangements for you because the amounts could be important. Say half a percent on every transfer into and out of the account. You use your contacts and influence with the bank to keep us out of the picture."

Charles Farrugia rubbed his free hand across his forehead and asked the question he had to ask: "OK Jérôme, how much do you mean when you say 'important'?"

Jérôme replied casually. "Oh, I dare say we are talking thirty million and upwards, maybe fifty million. Dollars of course, in case you think we're talking Yen."

"And all clean as a whistle no doubt?"

Jérôme laughed. "Have we ever sent you anything dodgy?"

"Not that I know of," replied Charles. "How come you three suddenly got so rich?"

"Give me a break Charles, its not our money, we're just salaried bankers and George works in a bar for God's sake."

Charles smiled "I'm going to have to note the file with something and I've got to have a sensible, and preferably true story for the bank."

"Its above board Charles, you'll be able to see that yourself because ninety percent of the proceeds are going to charity. Us three have been commissioned to collect funds from some very wealthy clients and acquaintances, put them in one pot and then distribute them to various worthy causes. No bank is going to fuss about that. You can even mention the charitable purpose of the company in the statutes."

Charles was being more difficult than usual. Jérôme frowned.

"Sorry to seem difficult," said Charles, echoing his thoughts, "but why two companies and why ninety percent for charities? Why not one hundred percent?"

Jérôme relaxed. "That's simple Charles and you know the answer. You just want to give me a hard time don't you?"

"Silly me, the other company is for you and will collect ten percent of all funds remitted to cover your outgoings and commissions."

"Yes, that's right. I'll tell you all the ins and outs one day but right now we are going to be working our arses off for several months."

"That will make a change."

"Charles. Fuck off."

"Not just now thanks, but don't worry Jérôme, I can get this done. Speak soon."

Jérôme hung up and went through to Lucas' office. The process had begun. He sat down in front of his computer and opened Microsoft Word to concentrate on his second task, a fake letter from TRACFIN* making enquiries about a certain Pablo Jimenez. The sort of letter that would make any banker tremble and shake like a Chihuahua trapped by a giant python.

---

* *TRACFIN is the French anti-money laundering authority*

HANS TEUBER

HANS TEUBER WAS NOT DISSATISFIED. He sat back in his chair at the breakfast table, the sound of the toaster popping up provoking a Pavlovian rush of saliva. The best moment of the day, the best meal of the day he chortled inwardly.

The table was littered with butter, jams, slices of cheese and Spanish sausage, a bowl of fruit and a large pot of coffee.

Hans Teuber enjoyed his solitary life and enjoyed the feeling of immense security as he contemplated the size of his bank account.

He skimmed through the newspaper and then turned on the television. More boring stuff about Iraq. Well, they could invade the place as far as he was concerned. Nothing they did over there would have any impact on his snug little existence in Liechtenstein.

He had done well indeed. Only sixty and retired with a generous pension and some thirty five million dollars in safe totally liquid investments. If you wanted to be rich what more logical place to work in than a bank?

He was surprised but not alarmed when he heard a knock at the door. He rose to his feet, wiped some butter off the side of his mouth and wrapped his dressing gown more tightly round his expansive waist. Probably the postman with another batch of the second hand porn DVD's he'd ordered through Ebay. He opened the door.

"Good morning Hans."

Hans Teuber was very taken aback. Not only had he not seen Lucas for over ten years but also he found him very changed. Not physically, apart from the fact he seemed rather more muscular. No, there was something threatening and insolent about him as he leant against the door frame. And there was a younger man with him who looked dangerous. In fact who looked murderous. A hoodlum.

"Lucas, I can't believe my eyes."

Lucas pushed his way in, followed by the hoodlum, and closed the door behind him. "You're not going to believe your ears either."

48

Hans Teuber's adrenalin levels shot up about 100%. His pulse increased and he felt that slightly worrying pain in his chest which he'd been putting off going to the doctor about.

"What's happened?" He asked breathlessly.

"I've been approached by TRACFIN Hans. They were wondering if I knew anything about your friend."

"What are you talking about? What friend?"

"Don't you have any friends Hans? You didn't consider Pablo a friend?"

Lucas held up the TRACFIN letter which Jérôme had so masterfully fabricated on his home computer.

Teuber's chest pain increased. The hoodlum stood a couple of metres away.

Lucas took a step forward. "Yeah, Pablo, your friend, not mine. You opened a big account for him and you did some very big transfers for sure, not to mention stuff he must have kept in his safety deposit box. So I just wanted to check what you want me to say to the TRACFIN guys."

Teuber sat down and stared at Lucas with disbelief. How could he be so callous and hostile? What had he done to Lucas? Well, there was the small matter of the vanishing three million dollars but he was convinced he had persuaded Lucas that he had nothing to do with it. It had all been Gerhardt's wrongdoing. They had agreed at the time that it was impossible to do anything about the theft. You couldn't go to the police about stolen money, the origins of which were so clearly criminal, without getting locked up yourself.

"This is outrageous. What do you mean? How can you possibly threaten me in this way? You were the one who introduced me to Pablo Jimenez...."

He stopped talking as the hoodlum raised his eyebrows and took a step towards him. Teuber's square face was already soaked in sweat.

"Agreed," said Lucas. "But it was an innocent introduction Hans. He didn't figure on any of the World Check lists, we both just thought Liechtenstein could help sort out a few tax problems for him when he invested those twenty five million. Then the news hit the front pages about the drug cartel, the murders, the political connection with Noriega in Panama and you did fuck all about informing the authorities. You just sat on those millions, doubtless with the help of Gerhardt who I'm sure had his usual power of attorney. And then Jimenez was murdered. Now what is it that makes me think you kept the money for yourselves?"

Lucas stared at his victim, inscrutable and pitiless. The medicine seemed to be working. Hans Teuber was trembling. The hoodlum smiled cynically.

"Do you know what happens to people like you when TRACFIN gets its claws in? Prison, big time, followed by total social ostracism when you get out. Not to mention confiscation of all assets. Just think of your savings Hans, all disappearing in a puff of smoke."

"What do you want from me for God's sake? I thought we were partners."

"We still can be Hans. But partners have to share things. Money and information for example."

Teuber stared at Lucas with a fresh wave of panic. "Surely you're not going to ask me for my money? I'm retired Lucas, I don't have much and you're way out of line regarding Jimenez."

"As a matter of fact I am. Going to ask you for money that is. And I'm also going to ask you where Gerhardt is. And I'm only going to ask you once."

Teuber stared at the muscular man in front of him, took in the expression in his eyes, looked at the hoodlum standing nearby and started blubbing. Lucas slapped him hard once, waited for him to start to recover from the shock and then slapped him a second time, harder.

"*Oh mein Gott,*" Teuber whimpered.

Lucas took off his tie and slipped it round Teuber's fat neck. He started pulling it tight, waiting for the panic. Then he let the fat man fall to the floor, gasping for breath.

Lucas stood above Teuber with a heavy foot on the man's chest. The hoodlum walked over and pulled out his revolver, pointing it at Teuber's head.

"I think we are in agreement now. Twenty five million plus interest, call it thirty million, plus precise details of Gerhardt's whereabouts and you're free. You've got three seconds before my friend loses his patience."

Teuber's eyes bulged with horror. He nodded his head and just managed to whisper through his bruised throat.

"What are my guarantees? How do I know you won't come back and blackmail me again?"

Lucas took his foot off the man's chest. He had won. The hoodlum spat on the floor and put his gun back in his pocket.

"Very simple Hans. As soon as you make the payment you will be linked forever to me. You denounce me and you denounce yourself. I denounce you and I denounce myself. Nice guarantee for both of us."

Hans Teuber scratched his head for a moment. He was still coping with too many emotions to be able to grasp Lucas' inexorable logic.

"Oh, one last thing Hans. If for whatever reason you forget to make the payment you will have the pleasure of seeing my friend again." Lucas nodded in the direction of the hoodlum and slapped a piece of paper down on Hans' breakfast table with the bank references and account number of the newly created Seychelles company provided by Charles.

"And if you warn cousin Gerhardt that we have his address you will also see him again. And I can assure you he will be the last thing you see in your life. Not a pretty sight."

The hoodlum stood by looking bored and scratching the stubble on his chin.

Hans Teuber struggled to his feet and found paper and pencil to note down his cousin's address.

THE PLAN

///

"JESUS, YOU EVEN SCARED ME THERE," said George as he sat back in the VW Passat they had hired for their expedition to Liechtenstein.

"Yeah, I had to force myself a bit, I don't like slapping people, not even scum like Hans Teuber. But you have to admit, it worked like a dream."

"It did, it was incredible. Did I look good?"

Lucas laughed. "Good? You looked so much the part it was awesome. I swear to you, you were scary."

****

George had arrived at the bank shortly after 10.00h, exactly a week earlier. Lucas' secretary, Solange, had greeted him warmly. There was a tacitly understood attraction between the two which neither wished to bring too close to the surface. Not for the moment anyway.

"Your brother is waiting for you George," she smiled. "Can I get you a coffee?"

"Essential," replied George. "That's why I came this morning. *Café à la Solange*, every man's desire." Solange giggled.

George had swallowed far too much caffeine already but he loved the way Solange made him feel at home. And he loved the discreet flirtation as she bent over to put the coffee on the table. She had even given him a little wink once when she had placed some biscuits on the table. Biscuits, crumpet. Silly thoughts.

She had showed him into Lucas' office.

Lucas was on the telephone and Jérôme got up to shake his hand. They liked each other and had got to be friends during the course of countless evenings spent at Lucas' house in Chateauneuf.

When Lucas had at last hung up, he sat down and outlined his plan which was, according to him, brilliant by its sheer simplicity.

"We all agree that we should at least get our three million Dollars back? And piss on Gerhardt Teuber's face?"

George and Jérôme both nodded.

"OK, this is how we do it. Gerhardt's cousin Hans is, as you know, a fat old man who thinks he's got it made and that he's pulled the wool over our eyes. He's sitting on tens of millions in my view. He's had such a cossetted life he won't be able to resist the slightest pressure. So we are going to scare the shit out of him by blackmailing him with a TRACFIN enquiry which we, of course, invent. Jérôme, you can manufacture some TRACFIN headed paper?"

Jérôme nodded again, dubiously.

"The supposed enquiry will relate to Pablo Jimenez, the international crook and ex-leader of the Panamanian drug cartel. We will convince Teuber that if he doesn't cough up our cash and tell us of Gerhardt's whereabouts we will denounce him as the person who opened Jimenez's account. George will come with me, dressed and looking and smelling like a gangster. Hans will do exactly as we say to avoid prison and /or death."

George and Jérôme looked at each other and then laughed with disbelief.

"Lucas old chap," said George incredulously. "You simply can't be serious. What have you been smoking?"

Lucas continued, unperturbed: "Jérôme will do his usual clever stuff setting up an offshore company for us, two in fact, and our friend Hans is going to make a mighty transfer to one of them. I want all of our three million plus all of what I estimate to have been stolen from the now deceased, may god bless him, Pablo Jimenez. Stage two is going to be more or less the same operation with Gerhardt."

George intervened. "So when you've relieved Hans of several tens of millions of dollars, you just say *aufwiedersehen* and the dear little chap waves goodbye and sheds a tear or two?"

"He can't do anything. Any misbehaviour and he knows you'll be back to knock him off and any sneaking to the authorities leaves him in the shit as an accomplice." Lucas allowed himself a tiny smile of satisfaction.

Jérôme looked up. "Pablo Jimenez was a very rich man Lucas. When you met him and referred him on to Hans, how much was he talking about? How much did he need to bank?"

"Twenty five million," replied Lucas smoothly.

More silence, punctuated by sighs from Jérôme.

George stood up. "This is absurd. But I'm in."

"*Patron*," said Jérôme. "If it works do we keep it all?

Lucas shrugged. "Let's face it Jérôme, neither of us needs any more money. I recommend we keep what we lost to Gerhardt and give the rest away. Some kind of charity linked to Bosnia?"

****

"OK," said George, as they left Liechtenstein and the VW reluctantly picked up speed on the motorway. "So I was scary, and God knows why but I take that as a compliment, and that was a mind blowing experience. But there is still something a bit surreal about all of this...."

"That's a good word," said Lucas.

"Eh?"

"Surreal."

"OK, shall we dumb things down a bit?"

"Go on," said Lucas.

"Fucking unbelievable."

"Let's have a drink."

"I thought you were supposed to have given up drinking?"

"You'd drive a saint to drink."

They pulled up at a *gasthaus*. As they ordered a beer Lucas extracted a scrap of paper from his pocket.

"What's written down here George?" He asked.

George studied it. "An address. Somewhere in Costa Rica."

"Our next destination. Gerhardt Teuber's pad is in Costa Rica. Better get out your sun tan lotion."

George stared out of the window of the *gasthaus* shaking his head.

"Did I say 'surreal'?"

"Remember what I told you in the wine cellar. Revenge, punishment. We're not going to live like pigs in shit any more. We're going to nail Gerhardt. Nothing surreal about that."

They clinked their glasses.

THIRD PARTY

JOHN BRADEN and his colleagues had worked as a team within the CIA for seven years. They specialized in money laundering and knew more about its sordid sources than almost anyone on the planet. But they didn't know everything. And what they didn't know they assumed was what the powers that be didn't want them to know. The trails they followed took them uncomfortably close to some very powerful institutions.

When they came across a trail that started heating up and were suddenly given another assignment they shrugged their shoulders and deduced that they had sailed too close to the wind. The wind was scary. They didn't know where it came from exactly.

Iraq had been a case in point. Monies transiting around the offshore world and oiling the wheels of the illegal arms trade had led to some astounding conclusions as to who was supplying Sadaam Hussein.

The suppliers were looking alarmingly close to home but they delivered their goods through such a labyrinthine chain of intermediaries that they could not be accused of having knowingly done any wrong. How could they have known that their legal and fully vetted client, situated in one of the aligned countries, was going to sell on the merchandise to a rogue state?

It was not worth thinking it all out. The system was the system. Braden's masters would decide, for example, to arm the Muhadjin in Afghanistan to help them conquer their soviet oppressors and then the former, having got rid of the latter, would turn on their supposed benefactors and provide cover for and nurture Al Qaeda. And then the Marines got blown to pieces by the weapons supplied by their Commander in Chief.

The fact was that everything was imploding in its own web of lies, contradictions and Machiavellianism. Once one had understood that, one had understood everything. No more ideals, just work to the rules of those who paid you. Everything, ultimately, was corrupt.

Iron had entered into Braden's soul. But he still thought his job was worthwhile, despite all the contradictions and constraints.

He forgot about his doubts when his secretary came in with the list of red flags and a coffee. Red flags were automatically generated and attached on the computer listings spewed out of the surveillance systems tracking money flows across the world.

Hundreds of millions of transactions took place every day so the only way to make the listings comprehensible and useful was to filter them down to a series of categories: offshore centres, those above ten million dollars, those emanating from accounts already under surveillance, those which were of a repetitive nature, those which originated from or were destined for beneficiaries with accounts in "bad banks" etc. Braden could shift the parameters as he wished.

He smiled at his secretary, thought for a second how depressing it was that he barely watched her well-shaped bottom as she walked out of the door, let alone contemplated getting near it, and started speed- reading the list.

NICE ARRIVALS

///

KRAZICEK SAT COMFORTABLY in his window seat, sipping his Vodka & Tonic and stared out of the Air France Boeing 747. The flight from Dubai had been uneventful but exciting all the same. Exciting because he was starting out again, exciting because the French airhostess assigned to the Club class cabin was sexy and clearly not indifferent to his charm and exciting because he was out for blood. Blood and money.

The approach to Nice was spectacular. The « Mistral » was blowing strongly from the West so the sky was clear and the sea whipped up. Palm trees, just visible, resisted bravely, refusing to let go of their foliage despite the brutal onslaught from the wind.

The plane banked over Cap Ferrat and headed back towards the landing strip, obliged to land into the wind. He looked down on the Promenade des Anglais on his right and it all seemed so familiar. How many times had he seen pictures of this, how many times had he planned to come to the Côte d'Azur? After all, through some weird quirk in his parents' itinerary through life they had been obliged to stop in Nice for the birth of the twins. So in a way this was back to roots.

He heard the ice clink and roll in his glass and resumed his study of the airhostess' body. Just as good from behind as from the front. A rare thing indeed. He wrote on the back of a little paper mat supplied with his drink, *Jon Vanhouteghem*, the name he had adopted on one of his three false passports, together with the name of his hotel, *L'Hermitage Monaco*.

As the hostess swished past performing her last checks before landing he caught her hand, gave her the paper mat and, with a not unattractive smirk, looked the other way.

****

Jon Vanhouteghem checked into the Hermitage Hotel in Montecarlo and found it OK but not quite to his liking. It just seemed a bit isolated from the Casino Square epicentre. In a microcosm like Monaco, a few hundred metres meant the difference between being at the heart of the principality and just missing the feel and the action.

He decided to stay for the night in case the air hostess rang and then move to the Hotel de Paris which was right on the square. Both hotels belonged to the same company, *Société des Bains de Mer*, and the change from one to the other would be simple.

He stretched out on his bed and hesitated between a large Vodka and Tonic and going to work out in the hotel's gym. He chose the latter, summoning a bit of willpower. His physical condition was superb. Mustn't let it go.

Before changing he sat down at the desk in his room and extracted a sheet of notepaper. He wrote down a short list of priorities :

1/ Air hostess

2/ Bank, Jérôme, Liechtenstein ?

3/ Who pulled the trigger?

Never lose sight of essentials Krazicek. Your elder Brother Vuk, who was born about one minute before you, taught you that.

He tried to imagine who might have got the better of his invincible sibling.

SHE WHO PULLED THE TRIGGER

AMRA WAS NOW TWENTY eight years old. Her youthful beauty had not been diminished by her years of work in Bosnia. It had deepened.

When she had arrived in 1996 she had three million dollars in her pocket and a mission in her mind which was all consuming. Her slaughtered family had been avenged when she had pumped Vuk, their murderer, full of bullets. So now she had to move on. Her tragedy was not the only one, there were thousands of others and she was going to help, try and help, somehow.

The devastated landscape and town of Sarajevo provided an obvious and forlorn metaphor for her own state of mind. Despite the miraculous recovery of Faruk, her brother and sole surviving close family, her return to Bosnia had furnished a constant daily reminder of the loss.

She travelled up and down the country, contacted the international aid agencies, helped the most impoverished and hopeless victims of the war directly by paying for clothes, food and lodging. Soon she became known in Bosnia's embryonic democracy as a force for good.

But burning racial hatred in Bosnia did not seem to be being replaced by an overwhelming desire for peace and harmony. Serbs, Croats, Bosnian Muslims, everybody had suffered. Somehow they had to find a way to cross the ethnic and religious barriers and cohabit as they had before.

"God I hate religion."

She smiled as she remembered when George had said that, a few days after Vuk's demise. They had made love urgently, as if the end of the world was nigh and afterwards, the fire in their loins temporarily assuaged, had talked about the future. Her future. George had wanted her to stay, made a tearful declaration of love, but she had explained why she could not, why she had to return to her homeland.

"Why did you suddenly say that, about hating God?" she had asked.

George had been silent for a moment, thinking about his discussion with her brother, Faruk, when they had so disagreed, the latter announcing his faith, George his total disbelief. He didn't want to go through it all again.

"You know, I had a long talk with Faruk about religion. We don't have the same views as you can imagine. But anyway, to answer your question, I said that because every time people start killing each other it seems to have something to do with not believing in the same God."

Amra sighed. "I just said I have to go back to Bosnia. That's got nothing to do with God or religion. I'm going because it's the right thing to do."

"Yeah, but if there hadn't been the Muslim divide with the Christians maybe Bosnia would have coped with the other problems, the ethnic and political stuff, and they wouldn't have started slaughtering each other. And you would have stayed with me."

Amra put her hand out. And the conversation had ended.

Shortly afterwards she had left Nice and joined Faruk's friend, Saleh, in Sarajevo. Saleh had wanted to marry her but she had turned him down.

So now she was on her own, on a mission, but the woman in her had a yearning, suffered from a loss somewhere deep down. And when she thought of George, all these years later, the need to see him and the sense of desire were accentuated.

She pursed her lips resignedly. There was another meeting with the U.N. representative, Peter Dyson, to take place that afternoon. She had taken on an informal reporting role with him. She refused to be employed or paid, she said she didn't need money and she didn't want to have any official status that might compromise her objectivity.

Peter Dyson, the envoy, relied almost exclusively on her as time went by. He had enormous difficulty understanding the complexities of post civil war Bosnia Herzegovina and his dispatches back to Geneva would have been limited and defeatist had he not been influenced by Amra's passion and vision. She seemed to be the only person in this mad Balkan universe who could rise above the partisan folly and elaborate ways for the UN to help achieve cohesion. But she was demanding.

"You want us to be some kind of *Deus ex machina* Amra. There is a limit to what we can do. A limit to what we can understand," Dyson had said one day.

"Peter, find another word for *'Deus,'*" she had replied. "I have a friend, a special friend, who says he hates God in all his elected forms. Understandable when you see what's happening here."

"Yeah, I get that Amra, but are they going to get it, the citizens of this country, that's the question? Are they going to understand they have to forget about their different gods and just build peace?"

"We all get it. I remember at school being taught the difference between relative and absolute value. When you are in the desert and your lips are parched and your body is turning into a piece of sandpaper and you're dying from dehydration imagine having to choose between a ton of gold and a simple glass of water. What's absolute value and what's relative?"

"So you think they are going to get that? Forsake the dogmatic crap and opt for survival? Look ahead and not backwards?"

"They'll have to. The fanatics will run out of traction one day. Normality will be the real dream."

TOOTH FOR A TOOTH

KRAZICEK GROUND HIS TEETH twice the day following his arrival in Monaco. The first time was when the airhostess proved more creative in bed than he expected and conjured a massively strong orgasm out of him.

He looked at her glistening body and dishevelled hair. It was always surprising when women proved that they wanted sex as much as men, it went against the grain of his ideas. Refreshing and disconcerting at the same time.

"Jesus!" he exclaimed. "Is that why you tell your passengers to fasten their seat belts?"

"Gives 'taking off' a whole new dimension doesn't it?" She replied, looking pleased.

Once was enough at that level of intensity he thought. Anyway, she had to leave for a New York flight. They were both flushed with the pleasure of their intimacy. A good moment to say goodbye, leave each other feeling hungry for more at a later date.

She had left by 11.00h and Krazicek had the pleasure of sipping another vodka and tonic alone in bed as he listened to CNN. Things were hotting up quickly in Iraq. He'd done well to get out.

The second time he ground his teeth was when he saw the third item on his list of priorities.

Who the fuck was it? Vuk was too strong, too clever to be killed by anyone. How was it possible? Now that he was focussed on finding the killer, the inner rage which had simmered for so long was fast heating up to boiling point.

The rage was mixed with guilt. He should have acted quicker at the time while the trail was still warm.

Whoever it might be, he would find him and kill him. That much he owed to Vuk.

MEET IN SAN JOSE

///

LUCAS LOOKED OUT of the passenger window of the Delta Airlines aircraft as it descended towards San José. When the plane banked towards the airport he caught a glimpse of the city and the backdrop of mountains and greenery. It looked surprisingly similar to the mental picture he had always carried of South and Central America: pockets of cheaply built and dirty urban sprawl couched in a vast and luscious tropical landscape.

He felt excited and he felt confident. He prodded his newly acquired abdominal muscles and made what he imagined was an irresistible James Bondish wink at the airhostess. She walked briskly by with apparent indifference. Lucas shrugged.

The aircraft touched down, taxied to the terminal and within minutes he found himself walking into the heat and humidity of a Costa Rican summer evening. He ran a finger round his neck to feel the sweat which had broken out. He felt strangely uplifted. He was on a mission on the other side of the planet. This was an adventure and he was going to enjoy himself. He would enjoy tracking down Gerhardt Teuber, he would enjoy the local flora (and fauna he thought) and he would allow himself an occasional high with the country's legendary "Centenario" rum.

He waited patiently at passport control and listened to the soft Spanish buzz. No hurry. Then he picked up his luggage, bought two and a half million Costa Rican Colons against five thousand dollars and stepped outside the airport to find a taxi.

"El Gran Hotel por favor," said Lucas, doing his best to roll his rs. The driver bustled round to open the rear door, smiled a warm *"Bienvenido a Costa Rica"* and started the old diesel engine. A cloud of black fumes pumped out from behind the vehicle as it fused with the traffic heading towards downtown San Jose.

****

As agreed between them, George had taken a later flight. Lucas had left on a Delta Airways flight to New York where he picked up a connection to San Jose. George had gone to Gatwick and taken British Airways to Miami followed by an American Airlines connection.

He felt a similar elation to that of his elder brother as he landed in San Jose, a mere hour later. Nice seemed so far away and he also felt a guilty sense of relief to be free from Nathalie and the endless arguments over what to do with his money.

When he arrived at the Gran Hotel he was delighted to see Lucas already settled at the terrace bar, which gave onto the Plaza Mayor. He was sipping fruit juice and busy chatting up the waitress.

George sneaked up from behind and put his hands over Lucas' eyes.

"No hay que creer ni una palabra de lo que dice mi hermano!" He said to the waitress.*

*"Que alegria, es Vd. su hermano? Encantada y bienvenido al Gran Hotel."***

She looked at George, gave Lucas a wink and moved to another table.

Lucas looked up and smiled happily. "George, I think we're going to have fun here."

"What kind of fun are you talking about Lucas?"

"Good, basic, harmless fun."

"Right."

Lucas caught the eye of his waitress again. *"Oye Princesa, una cervesita para mi hermano y....."*** He stared disapprovingly at his fruit juice,*"una mas para mi!"*

---

* *"You musn't believe a word of what my brother is saying*
** *"Oh great, are you his brother? Pleased to meet you and welcome to the Gran Hotel."*
*** *"Excuse me Princess, bring a little beer for my brother......and another one for me*

"Sod the orange juice, eh?" Said George.

When the beers arrived they lifted their glasses.

"To a successful outcome," said Lucas.

They swallowed the beer thirstily and ordered two more.

"You remember what Dad used to say when he was teaching us Spanish?" Asked George.

Lucas raised his eyebrows inquisitively.

"Salud, Pesetas y amor sin suegra."

"From the look of my little waitress," replied Lucas, "I don't think she's going to be introducing me to any potential mother in law."

They laughed, downed their second beer and agreed to have a recuperative siesta before hitting the town that evening.

---

* *"Good health, money and love without a mother in law"*

UNEXPECTED VISITOR

KRAZICEK PUT HIS NEW MOBILE TELEPHONE down and sighed with satisfaction. At last he had a lead. He had called all the British banks, asking to speak to Jérôme, the only name which Vuk had carelessly (or voluntarily?) mentioned in his letter.

In one bank, Barclays in the Rue Alphonse Kerr, there had indeed been a Jérôme but when he had been put through he quickly established that this was not the Jérôme he was seeking; a young wimpish voice had nervously announced that he was a trainee and Krazicek hung up.

He had then started calling banks at random, concentrating on the larger branches of French banks in Nice. Someone at the famous *Société Génerale* branch on the Avenue Jean Médecin (famous because a certain Mr Spagiari had tunnelled into the vault back in 1976) had said the only Jérôme she knew of worked with Banque Helvas.

Now Banque Helvas was not one that Krazicek had heard of but he deduced from the name that it was Swiss. And a Swiss bank would have been a natural port of call for Vuk.

He called and waited impatiently for the polite formula for taking incoming calls to finish: *"Bonjour, Banque Helvas, Solange Roumian à votre service, en quoi puis-je vous aider?"***

"Good morning, actually I'm thinking about opening a bank account but I need a British manager, one with private banking experience. I was told you have one together with an English speaking assistant. I think his name is Jérôme."

He listened to Solange's pleasant laugh. "You are very well informed Sir, that is exactly the situation. Would you like to make an appointment with Jérôme initially? I'm afraid Mr Watt, who's the manager, is on holiday, travelling."

** *"Good morning, Banque Helvas, Solange Roumian speaking, how can I help you?*

Krazicek's ears pricked up. "That's the name I was given. Michael Watt if I'm not mistaken?"

"Lucas Watt," replied Solange.

"Thank you, when is he back?"

"About two weeks, he's going to call me when he firms up on his return."

Krazicek frowned. He was so close now that he wanted to move in immediately.

"Thank you again, I will call back for an appointment with Jérôme later in the week."

He put the phone down and considered his options. Maybe it would be better to get to Jérôme initially. Vuk had said he was the one most involved in the transportation of the cash. He would know exactly where it was stashed. But Lucas Watt was probably the brains behind the whole operation.

He suddenly realised that he was acting too impulsively. He needed to develop some kind of strategy. And he needed to establish what links, if any, existed between the bankers and Vuk's death. He would never believe that Tomas, the alleged killer, would have got the better of Vuk. Something else had happened, but what?

He placed a piece of paper in front of him and wrote down the elements at his disposal: Lucas Watt, Jérôme, Banque Helvas, Liechtenstein.... As he wrote the last word his eyes narrowed. He'd found Banque Helvas, maybe he could find the bank in Liechtenstein.

Or to be more precise, maybe he could find the person who had dealt with Jérôme when he delivered the cash. Maybe things could be simplified.

Whatever. He just knew he was making progress.

****

He opened his laptop and started to read about Banque Helvas.

Banque Helvas is at the very heart of the Swiss banking system and is synonymous with tradition, solidity and sophistication.......

He stopped reading. He hated the complacent formulas and clichés. He googled Nice telephone directory and tapped in Watt. There was only one, a certain George Watt. He paused. Watt was an unusual name. Maybe there was a family connection. He noted the address and the telephone number. Then, spontaneously, he called. He waited for someone to pick up. A young female voice greeted him.

"Bonjour, Nathalie à l'appareil."

"Oh, er, good morning," he replied, sounding polite and hesitant. "I'm a friend of Lucas. May I speak to him?"

Nathalie made a sympathetic sounding laugh.

"You've got his brother's number."

Krazicek's turn to laugh: "Oh, George, right?"

"Yes, George. Lucas doesn't live in Nice any more and George took over his apartment. Maybe that's why you've got this number. I'll give you his new number....I guess you haven't seen Lucas for years then?"

Krazicek was drinking in all the new information. "Years and years. But I'm in Nice for a couple of weeks and I'd love to catch up with him and invite him to dinner. I've never met George so maybe I can meet him too."

"I'm afraid this is not your lucky day," Nathalie responded. "Both Lucas and George are away on business... business mixed with holiday I guess. They won't be back for a couple of weeks."

"I can't believe it."

"I'm really sorry....."

"Hey, don't worry, I'll change my plans if necessary." Krazicek decided to keep the momentum going. "Er, look, I guess you are a friend, maybe the wife of George. Would he mind if I asked you to dinner instead of Lucas. That way I can catch up anyway on his news. I'm completely on my own and at a bit of a loose end to tell you the truth. I've got business meetings coming up after tomorrow but until then......" He sensed her surprise and hesitation.

"Well, I don't know." Nathalie was genuinely taken aback.

"Sorry, just a spontaneous idea. It really doesn't matter, I don't know anyone that's all, meeting someone connected to Lucas would have been fun. Anyway lovely chatting and thanks for the telephone number."

Nathalie hesitated. He sounded really nice.

"Somewhere easy? We could meet if it was really early."

"You got it! That's really sweet of you." A tiny bit more treacle. "We can meet in half an hour, 18.30h. at *La Petite Maison*?"

Nobody would refuse an invitation to *La Petite Maison*. The concierge at the Hotel de Paris had told him about it.

"What's your name? You know mine. How will I recognize you?"

"The table will be reserved in the name of Jon Vanhouteghem. This early I guess I'll be the only person there. I'm looking forward to meeting you."

Nathalie felt a quiver of excitement. She didn't need to shower. Her hair was good. A touch of lipstick perhaps and that dress of hers which suggested more than it revealed. Then she knew she was ready for something more than dinner. She could taste the bittersweet premonition of betrayal in her mouth.

STRANGERS IN THE NIGHT

LA PETITE MAISON was the epitome of understated provincial snobbishness. You went there because it was famous, because the food was genuine *Niçois*, because it felt like the real thing, the quintessence of local gastronomic culture and tradition.

But unless you were part of the local elite (politician, notary, real estate magnate, imported pop star à la Elton John, or issue from an old and gracious Niçois family) you were treated by the manageress, Nicole, with a subtle blend of disdain and indifference which made you feel a trifle uncomfortable. That was why George never went there.

The big man sitting at a corner table in an otherwise empty restaurant did not look at all ill at ease. Nathalie noticed this immediately. In fact one or two waiters seemed to be almost standing to attention, waiting for him to choose from a wine list.

"Dom Perignon, super chilled," she heard him say. As the waiters rushed off she approached the table.

Jon Vanhouteghem rose to his feet. The same height as Vuk, with thick hair brushed back from his forehead above a virile and handsome face, he made any woman feel attracted. The underlying roughness and amorality did not show through. Except when he got angry and he certainly wasn't angry after he'd given Nathalie an appraising look. She was instantaneously under his charm.

He pulled a chair out for her. "This is so sweet of you to come to the rescue of a poor lonely man!"

'Poor lonely man' she thought to herself. This man wouldn't be lonely sitting on the moon.

"That's OK," she said carefully. How the hell was she going to control this situation? Did she want to? She sat down and Jon Vanhouteghem noticed the curve of her thighs.

Jesus, he thought to himself, talk about a sexual charge. This one is going to be as good as the airhostess. With the discreetest turn of his body he took off his jacket. He knew she would not be

71

able to resist lowering her eyes, even if only by a flicker, to see his maleness. And his maleness was already growing at an alarming rate. He sat down quickly.

"This is kind of weird. I haven't been on a blind date in my whole life! I know you want to get back early so let's order."

Nathalie smiled. Was she going to get back early? Unlikely, the way she was stirring deep inside.

"Something light for me," she said.

"Looking at the menu I reckon we've come to the wrong place if you want to eat light."

"Don't worry, salad and smoked salmon will be perfect."

Krazicek gave her an enigmatic smile. "I'll have the same as you." He watched the waiter pour out the champagne.

He raised his glass. Nathalie raised hers and held his provocative eyes.

MEANWHILE

%

LUCAS AND GEORGE walked out of the hotel and sniffed the midnight air. All the terrace tables were still full and the square in front was alive with hundreds of people, mostly young, a mixture of Costa Ricans and tourists. The atmosphere was peaceful but, to Lucas and George, carried a promise. They were going to have some excitement.

"So Lucas, you're the man running this show. You're the man about town, experienced, suave....."

"George, you don't need to be experienced or suave in this place. We are going to walk down that little street and stop at the first place that has a decent looking bar and some live music."

Lucas pointed to a narrow street, *Calle Balmes*, which sloped down to the left of the Gran Hotel.

He had taken a good decision. Within a few hundred metres of the hotel they found *"La Tortuga"*, a tapas bar cum discotheque with tables spilling out into the street and a large dance floor. A small band was playing. At least a dozen young girls were dancing on their own. All the men were seated, smoking and drinking beer.

George raised his eyebrows. "Fancy a drink or shall we go back to the hotel and read a book?"

They sat down near the dance floor and Lucas raised his hand to attract the attention of one of the waiters.

"Dos Cuba Libres por favor, mucha Cuba y poco Libre."* Lucas smirked a bit at his joke and settled down to study the general scene. Their drinks arrived.

George observed his brother. "You look like a randy old wolf Lucas. Can't you make it less obvious?"

"The one with the yellow skirt," Lucas replied.

---

*   *"Two Cuba Libres please, lots of 'Cuba' (rum) and just a little 'Libre' (Coca Cola)."*

George had already noticed the girl; about twenty-five years old, an exotic cocktail of local Indian, Spanish conquistador and a touch of African.

"So what are you going to do about it? Just sit and stare all night?"

"I'll show you," said Lucas. When the girl was facing their table he raised his glass, smiled directly at her and mouthed a few words of invitation. The girl smiled back, indicated she had a friend with her and Lucas smiled again and nodded.

"Jesus, we've only been here ten minutes Lucas. Are you sure you know what you're doing?"

"If you don't know what you're doing at my age you're in a bad way," Lucas replied. "And if you don't mind me saying, yours looks pretty tasty too."

The girls wended their way through the tables and stopped in front of theirs.

*"Que tal, de donde vienen?"**

"Hola, bien gracias. Somos cuidadanos del mundo! Y nos encantan las Costaricienses. Que van a tomar?" The girls giggled attractively and asked for Coke.***

The evening had got off to a promising start. George looked flushed and happy. Lucas very much the man of the world.

---

*   *"How are you doing, where do you come from?"*

**   *"Hi, we're fine thanks. We are citizens of the world! And we love the girls from Costa Rica. What are you having to drink?"*

BUSINESS AND PLEASURE

KRAZICEK DROVE FAST. He had crossed the Italian border by midday and the hired Porsche was now pointing north.

He thought back on the previous night. What a night it had been. Nathalie was astonishing, so much desire. When he'd managed to track down the Watt brothers he was going to tell George all the lurid details.

It had been pretty clear right from the start of course but he hadn't expected quite such a torrid session. Nathalie had accepted that last drink without batting an eyelid and he'd simply led her to his hotel, taken her to his room and asked her to undress, slowly please, while he sipped his champagne.

He put some music on and she performed a striptease. Very artistic in fact. Then he'd allowed her to undress him. She had gasped with delight when she saw the size of his prick and looked him unblinkingly in the eyes as she took him in her mouth.

When their passion had abated, at least temporarily, they had talked into the early hours of the morning.

"You going to be able to cope with this?" Krazicek couldn't give a damn but he wanted something, so better be nice. Also, the question led naturally to a wider inquisition. In the warmth of the bed.

Nathalie put her hand under the bedclothes and squeezed his testicles.

"Cope with that?"

Krazicek laughed warmly. "I know you can cope with that darling, what I want to know is can you cope with infidelity?"

"Don't worry about that, George pisses me off, he deserves this. He's so immature, so pathetic in some ways. I needed a real man."

"Why does he piss you off?"

"Everything," said Nathalie wearily. "He lives in some pseudo chivalrous mind-set which has nothing to do with today. He's a walking anachronism."

Krazicek listened with satisfaction. Keep up the act.

"Give me an example."

"Money," she replied.

Krazicek closed his eyes and sighed. "You told me he works in a bar or a restaurant or something. Maybe the poor guy simply hasn't got enough."

"That's the issue."

"What?"

"He has more than enough but he wants to give it all away."

"What ?"

"Yeah, well, it's one of those stories which are so unlikely you can't even tell anyone because nobody would believe you."

"Try me," he said.

****

And so bit by bit the story had unravelled. Krazicek's sympathetic ear and careful questioning encouraged Nathalie to reveal everything George had told her. The more she talked the more she found her new lover intelligent and comprehensive, charming and seductive.

"Sounds like an amazing story. You could make a film out of it. So when the shoot out took place on the Grande Corniche, who pulled the trigger, who actually killed this Vuk guy?"

Nathalie frowned for a second and then remembered the name. "Amra," she said. "She was the Bosnian girl, Faruk's sister. Tough little bitch apparently. I'm not sure George wasn't screwing her."

Krazicek laughed conspiratorially, hardly able to believe his luck. He was getting laid and finding out who had killed his brother at the same time. He felt his pulse quicken.

"George was screwing this Amra slut when he could have been screwing you? He must be out of his mind." He turned Nathalie onto her stomach and started caressing her buttocks. She opened her mouth and panted as she felt his penis harden in her hand.

Again? She was going to need a week to recover. He took her a bit more roughly than the previous two times, flattering her sense of her own desirability, pushing hard into her, making her come in a frenzy.

They lay back exhausted. After five minutes Krazicek got out of bed and made some coffee. They lit cigarettes.

"That was a spectacular night Nathalie. Thank you."

"Je vous en prie Monsieur."

They sat together for a few minutes, too tired to talk. But Krazicek was hoping, praying for that last bit of information.

"Weird, really weird when you think about it," he said.

"What?"

"The whole coincidence. That I should come to see Lucas and end up in bed with his brother's wife."

"Girlfriend," corrected Nathalie.

Krazicek smiled. "Girlfriend then. And that he should be in Liechtenstein on some mad campaign to track down some retired banker whose name he probably can't even remember, let's call him 'Herr Schmidt', just when I roll up and seduce his wife. Girlfriend I mean."

"Oh he knows his name. Hans Teuber, he was the manager of Baransteitbank and Lucas is convinced he was in cahoots with the other one, his cousin."

Krazicek put his hand on Nathalie's knee and smiled tenderly. "Let's forget the whole story for the moment and have breakfast. Champagne breakfast." Further celebration was needed.

Nathalie lay back happily. Krazicek felt exuberant. He observed her out of the corner of his eye and wondered if he felt anything. Maybe not, but he had to admit she was one hell of a girl.

ONWARDS

///

THE 4X4 TOYOTA was waiting for them outside the Gran Hotel at 10.00h the following morning. They had ushered the girls out of their rooms a couple of hours earlier with a handsome tip and repeated affirmations of their desire to return as soon as possible to see them again.

They finished breakfast on the terrace and signed the vehicle rental papers. Lucas took the wheel and nosed confidently out of the hotel and started negotiating his way round the Plaza Mayor.

"OK, so this is how it goes. You know I'm still a bit retrograde when it comes to the internet and all that?"

"Oh really?" Said George. "I never noticed." When Lucas was happy and feeling positive, he knew he had to unload one of his jokes. "I'm bracing myself Lucas, go ahead."

"It's not a joke so much as a parody. And it took me a bit of time to get it off pat."

"Spit it out Lucas, the suspense is killing me."

"OK, so you have to imagine this bloke trying to access some website and his password has expired:

Website: Sorry that password has expired - you must register a new one.

User: Did anyone discover that password and hack my computer?

Website: No, but your password has expired - you must get a new one.

User: Why then do I need a new one as that one seems to be working pretty good?

Website: Well, you must get a new one as they automatically expire every 30 days.

User: Can I use the old one and just re-register it?

Website: No, you must get a new one.'

"Is this autobiographical Lucas?" George interrupted.

"Let me finish."

User: I don't want a new one as that is one more thing for me to remember
Website: Sorry, you must get a new one.
User: OK, roses
Website: Sorry you must use more letters.
User: OK, pretty roses
Website: No good, you must use at least one number.
User: OK, 1 pretty rose
Website: Sorry, you cannot use blank spaces.
User: OK, 1prettyrose
Website: Sorry, you must use additional letters.
User: OK, 1fuckingprettyrose
Website: Sorry, you must use at least one capital letter.
User: OK, 1FUCKINGprettyrose
Website: Sorry, you cannot use more than one capital letter in a row.
User: OK, 1Fuckingprettyrose
Website: Sorry, you cannot use that password as you must use additional letters.
User:OK,1FUCKINGprettyroseshovedupyourassifyoudon'tgive meaccessrightfuckingnow
Website: Sorry, you cannot use that password as it has already been used

"I love it," said George appreciatively. They drove on for a few minutes, enjoying the strangely peaceful countryside.

"Right," said Lucas. "Stage two starts a bit more seriously. We're going to pay a little visit to our friend Gerhardt."

George frowned. "Great. But what makes you think he's going to be a walkover like Hans? Once again Lucas, I'm going to have to ask you what the plan is."

"The plan is being formulated."

"'Being formulated,'" George snorted.

"When you think about it it's better this way than the other way round."

"What?"

"Well, a lot of people focus on strategy and tactics and never properly formulate the final objective. We know what we want to achieve and that will enable us to improvise constructively as we go along."

"Bullshit. And what about the money? It's all very well saying 'fuck the money' but do you know what you're going to do with it?

"Steal from the rich and give to the poor."

"Nice one."

"I'm Robin fucking Hood and you're Little John. Little George."

George laughed despite himself. "As long as you don't think I'm Maid Marion I don't mind."

"Maid Marion was last night...."

"And I bet you gave her your silver arrow."

Lucas drove on, searching for a joke.

"Reminds me of why America is called 'America'."

"Go on."

"Well, when Christopher Columbus first landed there was a bunch of Indians hiding in the forest and one of them fired an arrow straight up his arse and he screamed *'Hay, marica!'* *...... since when....."

"Yeah, I got it." George looked out of the window of the jeep to hide his amusement.

The chaotic urban sprawl of San Jose had started to thin and within twenty minutes of leaving the hotel they found the first signposts for Guanacaste. Both men sighed with relief as the jeep picked up speed.

Lucas lit a cigarette. "So, how was your chicita?"

"Good," answered George laconically. "And yours?"

"Bad."

"Bad? But she was stunning."

"'Bad' like naughty."

"OK. I've taken some pictures to show Chloe."

---

*   *"Ouch, poofta"*

Lucas looked at his brother. "You're a fine one to talk! What about Princess Nathalie?"

"Yeah, I know. But to tell you the truth I'm a bit mixed up about her at the moment. It's like I needed some kind of change. Almost like I needed to settle a score."

Lucas raised an eyebrow and threw his cigarette out of the window. "Nothing to do with what I said when we drank all that wine?"

"Yes and no."

Lucas frowned. "Hey, I'm sorry about that. None of my business, I was just playing the elder brother, warning you. I may have been completely wrong. But I don't see the light of love in her eyes and I don't want a nice chap like you getting screwed......as in cheated."

"You said you didn't trust her. That was when I realised I had a similar feeling but I felt so guilty about it that I kept hiding it from myself." George scratched his nose, looking uncomfortable.

"I hope you haven't given her any details about the money."

San Jose was well behind them now and the landscape in front opened up. They were driving along flat plain land but there were clusters of soft green hills on either side. George avoided answering.

"What about you Lucas? Any feelings of remorse? If anyone deserves fidelity it's Chloe. She's so sexy anyway, even after three kids, I can't understand why you still need to get your leg over with anyone else."

Lucas looked relaxed. This was not an issue he was going to allow to trouble him, not since Chloe had withdrawn her warmth in bed.

"Come on Lucas, do you feel guilty?" George insisted.

"I can give you the long version or the short version."

"Ok, so give me the short version."

"No."

"No what?"

"No, I don't feel guilty."

"Well that's clear and to the point." George paused for thought. "And what about the long version?"

"No, absolutely not."

George sighed. Lucas carried on driving complacently in the direction of Tamarindo.

"Listen George, Chloe is my lawful wedded spouse and all that and I love her to bits, I'll stick by her to my dying day. But you know I've always had a healthy appetite and to be honest the dear girl has reduced physical contact .....dramatically."

"'Physical contact'? Never heard you use that particular euphemism."

"I just don't get my oats very often George. Ever since she gave birth for the third time. So the occasional straying from the straight and narrow is good for me and good for her."

Lucas did not want to tell George about the full extent of the love strike.

"OK," Said George

They entered a small village. On the left was a petrol station and small bar, apparently one and the same establishment.

Lucas slowed to a stop in front of the bar and looked at George. "Hair of the dog?"

They entered the welcome cool of the bar and ordered a beer. They drank out of the bottle and smiled as the barman/petrol pump attendant flicked the capsules expertly into a bucket some three metres away at the other end of the bar.

They said nothing for a few relaxing minutes until Lucas posed the question again, the one that had been nagging at him for years. "I don't know why I never asked you this but just how much of our story does Nathalie know? Did you tell her where your money came from?"

George looked uncomfortable again. "Well, not initially but then I couldn't hide it forever."

"Oh fuck," said Lucas.

There was a minute's silence as they both thought about the implications.

"How much does she know?"

"Pretty much everything. I'm sorry Lucas."

Lucas spoke quietly, with resignation. "You do realise you just said you didn't think you trusted her?"

It was George's turn to light a cigarette.

A DOUBLE WHAMMY FOR HANS

///

HANS TEUBER was still in a state of shock although the shock was slowly mutating into depression. Lucas and his hoodlum had reminded him of something which he had managed to hide from himself for most of his life: he was a coward. And his grovelling performance when Lucas had slapped him made him cringe with shame and embarrassment every time he thought about it.

One slap and he had given up 90% of his life savings. And there was nothing he could do about it. The money had gone and he'd signed the transfer instruction. And Lucas had him by the balls.

He thought about Gerhardt and realised he didn't even want to warn him, even if he'd been able to. Hans Teuber was not the sort of person to want to share good fortune and he had no objection to others suffering bad fortune, particularly when he'd suffered himself.

Fuck Gerhardt.

He settled down in front of the television to hear the latest on Iraq. He poured himself a large glass of cold white Porto. He felt momentarily comforted. A lot of people were getting bombed to hell but he was safe and sound in his apartment. He'd thought about changing to a new one but concluded it wasn't worth it. Lucas wouldn't be coming to see him any more.

So when there was a knock on his door while he was sipping his first early evening drink he was mildly curious but not alarmed. He put his slippers back on and waddled to the door. He peered through the spyhole and saw a face partially hidden by a baseball cap with DHL printed on the visor. Who the hell was sending him stuff by courier?

He opened the door.

Krazicek pushed him backwards so hard that he fell to the floor, momentarily losing consciousness as his head collided with the side of the glass coffee table. His hand caught his half finished glass of Porto, bringing it down to smash into pieces on the floor. One of the pieces lodged itself in his cheek, immediately provoking a spurt of blood which ran down his face and neck and was slowly absorbed by his shirt.

When he came to he found himself propped up against the wall with a wide piece of sticky tape across his mouth. Krazicek was pouring a glass of icy water over his head. Then he sat down opposite him on an armchair and started stabbing the cushioned armrest with one of the kitchen knives. Every time the blade pierced Hans Teuber winced. Every time he winced the more blood seeped out of his cheek. And when he saw the blood for the first time, soaking the front of his shirt, he thought he was certainly going to die.

Krazicek stabbed the armrest one last time and then stared at Teuber directly in the eyes.

"Do you want to stay alive?"

Teuber's eyes bulged as he nodded.

"Then don't make a sound."

Krazicek ripped the sticky tape off Teuber's chubby face. Teuber groaned and immediately received a blow on the side of his head. Through the dizziness and pain he just managed to prevent himself from screaming.

His intruder placed the knife on the coffee table and waited a few minutes.

"OK Hans. Hans Teuber. You can now start answering my questions. If you don't cooperate, or even if you do cooperate and I don't believe what you're telling me, I will start cutting little bits off you until there's nothing left."

Hans Teuber started nodding and blubbing at the same time.

"Tell me about Lucas, Hans."

Teuber's eyes, already wide with horror, widened further.

"Lucas Watt?" His voice was barely a whisper.

Krazicek nodded. "Everything you know, and in particular what happened when he came to see you last week."

Teuber tried to gather his thoughts as quickly as possible. If he didn't reply fast the man in front of him was going to start wielding that kitchen knife. He had no doubt whatsoever about it.

"He came uninvited. I hadn't seen him for years." He dabbed the cut on his face with the cuffs of his shirt but his arms felt like lead and it was all he could do to talk.

"Why did he come?"

"He claims I stole some cash from him which he'd left in the safe when I was working in Barantsteitbank."

"The cash belonged to Lucas?"

"Not even, it belonged to one of his clients."

"How much?"

"There were three million dollars."

Krazicek picked up the knife and studied the blade. "You just passed your first test Hans. Carry on like this and you may get out alive. One lie and I start using this. And then I bring in the dogs. They're in my car outside and they haven't been fed. Yet."

Krazicek watched Teuber crumble into an even more miserable heap.

"Do you like Dobermans?"

Teuber could only gulp. He didn't know what to answer. Krazicek approached with the knife. He held it just above Teuber's left ear.

"Yes."

"Good, I'll go and get them now."

"No."

"You don't like Dobermans? You don't like my dogs?"

"Please, please, I'm telling you everything."

"You've just started telling me everything." Krazicek stood up and slowly put the knife back on the coffee table.

"OK, the money belonged to a company, Panamanian, and the beneficial owner was a guy called Josef Havel. I never met him but I heard he got killed in some fight."

Krazicek felt a surge of genuine anger. His eyes narrowed and Teuber could see he was skating on thin ice. He hurried on.

"I don't know how it happened, I didn't know him."

"So when some poor guy gets shot you just steal his money. That's cool Hans."

"I, I......"

"You stole his money didn't you?"

Teuber stared miserably at the floor.

"You're a vulture Hans, some kind of sick ghoul." I always heard Liechtenstein was the arsehole of the world Hans, but you're the haemaroid on the arsehole. You deserved to be shot, not my brother."

"Oh mein Gott!"

Krazicek walked round Teuber's living room a couple of times and breathed out heavily.

"So where's the money?"

Teuber wrinkled his forehead. How was he going to explain the whole thing?

"I can give you as much detail as you want but the simple answer is Lucas stole it. He considered it his. I don't know why. He brought some thug with him, a guy with a revolver which he pointed at my head. He made me sign a transfer instruction, he made me transfer everything I had in my bank account to him."

"Everything?"

"Almost."

"How much did he take?"

"Thirty million dollars."

Krazicek whistled softly. This guy Lucas was not fooling around.

"What did he leave you?"

Teuber was still trembling like a rabbit and the idea of lying never entered his head. He just wanted to stay alive. "I've got about five million dollars left."

"Why should I believe that? How do I know you haven't got more?" Krazicek picked up the knife again.

"I swear to you, I can even show you my deposit confirmation."

Teuber suddenly had the germ of an idea. If this crazy murderous bastard standing in front of him was going to go after Lucas and the money he might just need Hans Teuber as a consultant.

"May I propose something?" He asked, his voice unsteady.

"You are not in a position to propose anything you fat piece of shit."

Silence fell as Krazicek started to stride round Teuber's living room for a second time. Teuber stared morosely at the floor, his cheek no longer bleeding but now throbbing painfully.

Very gingerly, very humbly, very obsequiously, Teuber said "I think I can help you."

Krazicek stared at him disdainfully. "How?"

Teuber gathered his thoughts and started carefully. "You want to track down Lucas right? For personal reasons because you think that one way or another he was linked to your brother's death or simply to get back your brother's money."

"He was linked," replied Krazicek. "It wasn't him who pulled the trigger. But I still haven't decided if he's going to go to hell with a bullet in his head. And I don't have to track him down, I know exactly where he works. So I don't see how you can help. So don't waste my fucking time."

Krazicek watched Teuber wilt.

But this was Teuber's last chance to try and salvage something from the nightmarish situation. His brain was now working efficiently.

"Please. Let me explain, I beg of you. Lucas has got my thirty million dollars and he's on his way to getting a lot more."

Krazicek at last showed some interest. "Go on. But don't make anything up or I'll slit your greasy throat and get the dogs."

Teuber winced yet again and felt his bowels loosen. He hurried on.

"Lucas wanted to find someone else, someone whom he knew was the person who really stole your brother's money........."

"Yeah, your cousin; tell me something new."

Scheiss, how come this psychopath was so well informed? Time to play his last card. "I know where he is and I know Lucas is on his way to beat him up, just like he did with me and then force him to transfer his money."

Krazicek laughed loudly. "Shit, you Teubers have been having a tough time."

"What I'm saying is I can be of help to you and we can maybe do to Lucas what he's done to your brother and me. And my cousin. Once he's got everything credited to his offshore company accounts we might be able to take it all back........"

Krazicek cut in: "Less of the 'we'."

Teuber apologized. "Forgive me, I'm sorry. I'm just saying that in exchange for my life I can point you in the direction of a lot of money. I know the name of Lucas' offshore company and I know where the bank account is. I had to sign the transfer instruction. I also know where my cousin Gerhardt is. I know a lot of stuff."

Krazicek looked at the fat German and had to admit he was beginning to make sense.

"I'm listening." Krazicek crossed his arms.

Teuber sat up slightly. "Lucas is in Costa Rica. That's where Gerhardt retired, near Tamarindo. He forced me to give him his address. There's nothing I can do, either about the money he stole from me or about Gerhardt. He's got something on me, he can get me thrown into prison on a money laundering charge. I'm stymied. I'll give you the details if you want......"

"Never mind the details," said Krazicek."Tell me about how we get the money and tell me how much this Gerhardt creep has got." He was beginning to get excited.

"Gerhardt must have the same as me. We kind of worked together."

"Interesting." Shit, he'd set off on a mission to track down Vuk's killer and pick up the three million dollars that had been left in the safe and he was going to end up with twenty times more. And thanks to Nathalie he knew who the killer was. Progress was a wonderful thing, it made you feel good.

"Keep talking Teuber."

"I have no doubt that Lucas is going to get Gerhardt's money. Gerhardt is just an out of condition crook who's going to be sixty five next year......."

"Funny that, he reminds me of someone else I know, someone who's sitting on the floor in front of me right now."

Teuber hesitated and then went on. "Well, anyway, in my opinion he's going to pull exactly the same trick. He'll scare the hell out of Gerhardt with his gangster friend......"

"What gangster friend?"

"A young guy, really vicious, he had a revolver which he held to my head when I was signing the transfer instruction."

Krazicek roared with laughter.

Teuber looked perplexed. "What, I mean why is that so funny?"

"Your gangster. You know who that was? It was George, Lucas' brother."

Teuber looked even more perplexed. "How do you know? How do you know so much about everything?"

"I'll spare you the intimate details Teuber, let's just say I've been screwing George's girlfriend while he's away with his brother playing cowboys and Indians."

For the first time a smile played on Teuber's face. "*Wunderbar, wunderbar!*"

"Carry on Teuber."

"Lucas is going to force Gerhardt to sign a transfer to his offshore company. There will then be at least sixty million dollars in the account. Now, as I was saying, I know the name of the company, I know the account number and I know the bank. It's a bank I've used in the past myself when helping out clients with tax problems.

"I also know how their security system works. All the clients have what is known as a digipass which they activate with a password. Then they tap in the amount of money they want to transfer or deposit or whatever and the digipass flicks up a code.

That code is noted on the physical transfer instruction, which can be sent by fax, and the bank then processes the transaction."

"So, if we have the digipass and the code we access Lucas' company account. Simple as that?"

"Yes," said Teuber.

"I'm listening Teuber."

"We don't know who else has signing powers, if the signatures are joint or single and we don't know what he might have set up as additional security. He's quite a tough guy and his brother is too. But I was thinking, you say you are, er, acquainted with his brother's wife. Will you be renewing contact with her?"

Krazicek stared at him. Devious little shit. He was going to be useful, that was for sure, but ultimately dangerous. Too clever for his own good.

"Yes. You think George might have a signature and a digipass?"

"If he has a digipass then you can be pretty sure that he has single signature authority on the account together with his brother and probably Lucas' assistant, a guy called......"

"Jérôme," interrupted Krazicek.

"Jérôme. Exactly," acquiesced Teuber, as ingratiatingly as possible. "If there was a joint signing arrangement then there would be only one digipass and you can be sure Lucas would keep it. Maybe in his office, maybe hidden at home.

"But if George has got it maybe his wife will be able to find it? Do you think she would cooperate, do you, well, do you have an amorous relationship, would she be tempted by the idea of helping to find the digipass and once found, together with the code, eloping with you?"

Krazicek walked round the living room again, stroking his chin. This grease ball wasn't just devious, he was fucking brilliant! Let Lucas do all the dirty work and then clean him out with the press of a few buttons. No bodies to dispose of and the purest of pleasurable sensations as he imagined Lucas' state of shock and incredulity when his money disappeared. And he wouldn't be able to do anything about it even if he managed to trace it.

If the digipass thing didn't work out he would simply resort to his slightly more heavy handed plan of hanging Lucas up by his testicles until he cooperated.

"OK Teuber, this is your lucky day. Here's the deal. You keep your money for the moment, what's left of it, and you stay alive. If it works out like you say and you help me get those sixty million dollars then you won't ever hear of me or from me again. If it goes wrong it will be your fault. You lose your money and I feed you to the dogs."

"Thank you," said Teuber, before he had time to realize it was the most ridiculous expression of gratitude he had ever formulated in his life.

LOVE IS IN THE AIR

NATHALIE'S HEART skipped a beat when she heard the voice on her mobile telephone. Krazicek had mumbled stuff about ships that pass in the night and how things were complicated. Typical evasive male tactics. But here he was calling her just two days later. Two days after that amazing night.

She tried to sound calm as her legs turned to jelly and her heart pounded.

"Well that's a nice surprise."

She could see him smiling down the airwaves.

"I'm glad to hear that, "said Krazicek. "I missed you. And then I needed to talk to you about something important."

Nathalie tried to digest what he was saying. "You missed me and you want to talk about something important. Are the two connected?"

"I guess so. I'm in Nice, at the same hotel. Will you come round?" Krazicek pursed his lips waiting for the answer.

"What, now?" Nathalie could barely conceal her joy.

"That's my girl. Room 505."

Nathalie put down her mobile and looked at herself in the mirror. Then she smiled at herself. God knows where this was going, but while it was going she was going to enjoy it.

She stepped under the shower and washed carefully. Then she put on clean underwear, transparent French lingerie that made the most of her firm breasts and accentuated her long slender legs, making a sensual focal point of her triangle. Light make-up, a dab of *eau de cologne*. Her eyes were clear and shone with youthful life. She was ready.

Krazicek waited for her impatiently. He'd thought long and hard about how to persuade her, about how much he could tell her. He was going to screw her arse off, that was for sure. Then he was going to test her somehow. See what she was really made of.

Certainly the way she had talked about George had revealed a toughness that contrasted with her youth and beauty. He thought about the night they had spent together again and felt an immediate stirring in his loins. And something else which disturbed him, although it was agreeable in a strange and unfamiliar way.

Nathalie arrived at the hotel. She took the lift to the fifth floor and found Krazicek's room at the end of the corridor on the left. Great, he'd taken a room with a sea view. She knocked on the door and stood quietly. She'd never felt so excited in her life.

"Welcome. Come in." They stared at each other. He pushed her gently onto the bed and started to pull off her skirt. Then he unbuttoned her blouse.

He stared at her young firm body, noted the lingerie and then undressed himself. They frantically explored each other's bodies until she pulled him, urgently, inside. She screamed as she came, a climax she had never imagined existed, so strong that she thought she might die.

Krazicek staggered out of bed to the minibar and pulled out two Vodkas and a bottle of Tonic water. She watched the muscles ripple in his athletic body and thought that this had to be paradise.

"I'm going to die with a smile on my face Jon, just thinking about what we did."

'Jon', of course. He wondered how long that particular identity would last.

"So what was the important thing you wanted to talk to me about? Can't be as important as the orgasm you just gave me."

Krazicek handed her the drink. "I don't know where to start. I'm still recovering from what *you* did to me."

"Start with whatever is easiest."

Krazicek pondered. "OK, how about this? I'm not Jon Vanhouteghem."

Nathalie looked puzzled. Maybe this was a joke. Then she saw the expression on Krazicek's face and saw he was being serious. Then she felt alarmed.

"What does that mean? Why should you use a false name with me? Are you not Jon?"

Krazicek was calm. "You told me a lot of stuff about Lucas and a guy called Vuk. You told me how Lucas got to be so rich. How his whole entourage got to be rich."

Nathalie frowned, now both alarmed and confused. "What's that got to do with anything?"

"Everything. I'm Vuk's brother."

Nathalie shrank back into the bedclothes. "That's not possible."

Krazicek pulled out a worn leather wallet from his trousers which were hanging on the back of a chair. He opened it and extracted a small passport sized photograph.

"Do you know who that is?"

Nathalie studied the image, curious despite her incipient panic.

"I guess it's you, it is you in fact, when you were a bit younger."

Krazicek paused for dramatic effect. "That's Vuk."

There was a long silence; Nathalie didn't dare look up. Then the panic started to surface. Her breathing quickened and she could feel the pulse in her neck.

Krazicek was the first to speak. "I don't know what's going through your mind exactly but you're probably wondering if I'm as dangerous as Vuk. You're probably wondering what I'm going to do to you. The answer is nothing. I just want to make a proposal."

Nathalie looked at him but not in the eyes. "Proposal? What kind of proposal? There's nothing I have and nothing I can do which could possibly interest you."

Krazicek squatted down by her and took her hand. She pulled back. She felt the terror rising again. This man could snap her in two with one hand.

"I'm sorry Nathalie, I've scared you. Listen, I'm not Vuk. Just his brother. I'm not the same person, I don't kill people, not unless one day I have to, and I'm not even remotely connected to what happened in Bosnia. Please believe that and then you'll be able to listen to my proposal."

"What's your real name?"

He smiled. "It's a weird one for anyone from outside Serbia. Krazicek."

"Krazicek," she repeated softly. "I like it."

"Impossible," laughed Krazicek. "I don't think it even officially exists.

"Encore mieux."

"Well, that's taken some tension out of the air! I think we'd better have a bit more to drink. I think I need it more than you. I've got this crazy proposal, like I said."

Nathalie kissed him. "Crazy like Krazi."

"You got it."

"Go on then. Try me."

Krazicek frowned with concentration. "Do you believe in destiny Nathalie?"

"Sort of."

"Sometimes things come together, you just have to recognize what's happening and act accordingly. It's like fate provokes some amazing coincidence but nothing will necessarily happen unless you make a move yourself."

"This is intriguing......Krazicek......I'm hooked." Nathalie sat up and took another sip from her Vodka. Now she had forgotten her panic she could relish the sublime decadence of the moment she was living. Late afternoon, not even early evening and she was having passionate sex with a stranger who carried a false name and plied her with alcohol. A fleeting image of George traversed her mind. She chased it away.

"Well this is the line up of events: I'm living in Baghdad earning a load of money selling stuff to Sadaam Hussein......

"What sort of stuff?" Nathalie asked, and then regretted the interruption.

Krazicek shrugged. "Stuff I shouldn't have been selling but which would have been sold by someone else if I hadn't done it. So

---

* *"Even better."*

96

there I was, getting rich, when all of a sudden there's 9/11 and Bush switches the spotlight onto Iraq. And then he decides to invade, or at least we know it's a foregone conclusion that he's going to invade. And that spells trouble for me. Particularly as I'm the guy who's selling the stuff Sadaam needs to fight a war."

Nathalie made a quick intake of breath.

"Yeah, I know. Naughty boy, you can slap my wrist. So I decide to get out and go and do what I should have done seven years ago."

"What was that?"

"Track down Vuk's killer and, even if I don't need it, recoup some of the money that was stolen from him. Matter of principle."

Krazicek watched as Nathalie's eyes widened and a look of fear came upon her again.

"So I get on a plane, fly here and thanks to one or two clues which Vuk left me, like his bank contact being English and working in Nice, I end up on the 'phone to you!"

He paused with amusement. "And then you start climbing all over me and I can't get rid of you because you never allow me to put my pants back on."

Nathalie kicked him gently. *Mon dieu,* this guy was an arms dealer and all she felt was lust. And the beginning of something else which was growing faster than she cared to admit. She hadn't registered the significance of Krazicek's words, nor that she had furnished Amra's name.

"Then you tell me a whole load of things which would have taken me ages to find out. I go to Liechtenstein....."

"What do you mean? When did you go to Liechtenstein?"

Krazicek was enjoying himself. "You remember you stayed in bed, the morning after the night before? You were out for the count. I was pretty washed out myself but I left you fast asleep and hired myself a car and drove to Liechtenstein to meet Hans Teuber."

Nathalie's expression of incredulity became even more accentuated. Yes, she remembered how disappointed she had felt waking up alone and then leaving the hotel to go back home.

"He agreed to meet you?"

"I didn't give him a choice. Now, listen to this. It's going to throw a whole new light on your perception of George. He and Lucas bust into Teuber's apartment, beat him up and threatened to shoot him if he didn't sign over all his savings."

"What?" Nathalie's position on the bed changed again. She swung her legs over the side and stared at the huge man aghast.

"Yeah, no kidding. He transferred thirty million dollars to an offshore company bank account. Looks like they got a whole load more than the three million which was stolen from the safe. Lucas and George got rich."

"This.....this is ridiculous. Neither Lucas nor George are capable of that."

"Maybe they're a bit tougher than you imagine. And I'll tell you something else." Krazicek paused. "They're in Costa Rica right now as you know, but not on a boys only surfing gig, they're on their way to bust Gerhardt. According to Hans he's got the same amount stashed away. So very shortly their thirty million becomes sixty million."

Nathalie suddenly burst into laughter. Uncontrollable laughter. Krazicek watched her with bewilderment. She laughed so much the tears started flowing and so infectiously that Krazicek started too.

When they stopped at last their complicity seemed complete.

"Krazicek, I love you. I mean it. Make any proposal you want."

Krazicek looked alarmed. Shit, surely she didn't expect him to marry her?

Nathalie read his thoughts. "Any proposal except wedlock."

Krazicek released an exaggerated sigh of relief. "OK, here we go. Hans told me all about the bank in Cyprus. The bank where the sixty million is going to be deposited. You access the account with a digipass and a code. I want you to find the digipass, find the code and then ride off into the sunset with me to live happily ever after."

Nathalie froze in disbelief. "That's your proposal?"

"Yeah, that's my proposal."

A LAST FLING?

LUCAS AND GEORGE arrived in Tamarindo in the early evening. They parked their Toyota outside the first hotel and walked into the reception area to book a couple of rooms. The "Vista del Mar" looked quasi colonial and had a huge bar restaurant adjoining the entrance hall. It looked perfect. It would have been but there were no free rooms and the receptionist indicated that the only place where one could find any was "El Bucanero" in Playa Grande.

Playa Grande was big, as its name suggested. Lucas gasped as they turned the last corner of the dusty track leading there from Tamarindo.

"This is the first time I've seen the Pacific. I'm fifty years old. What have I been doing with my life?"

"Drinking and fornicating Lucas, you know that. Doesn't leave much time or energy for tourism."

"Yeah, well, how about drinking and fornicating on the Pacific? Perfectly compatible."

George studied the view. The beach was endless, golden sand backing at least a hundred metres from the water line. Flocks of Pelicans flew overhead. Vast powerful waves rolled in and a couple of late surfers were carrying their boards in the direction of one of only two buildings in sight. A simple round structure surrounded by tropical flora and topped by a roof terrace. As they approached they could hear some latino music and read the sign hanging from the entrance.

"El Bucanero" was just above the beach hut category. Lucas paid for two rooms, a week in advance, and agreed to meet George on the terrace after a shower.

He arrived first and greeted the barman. He ordered beer and sat back to observe the scene. Most of the other patrons were close to his age, muscular and deeply tanned but carrying a belly. All of them were male, many were local apart from a group of obviously

American men who were leaning against the bar talking loudly about the waves.

After ten minutes Lucas realised they were talking exclusively about the waves. Depth, power, height, late or early breakers, how they compared to the Caribbean side of the country. Lucas felt a twinge of admiration, bordering on envy. A single, simple, all consuming and profoundly healthy passion. An almost spiritual fusion with the ocean. What was his passion? Money, women, wine? Not a great deal of spirituality to be found.

George arrived and they sat peacefully sipping their beer, listening to the roar of the sea and the soft music.

"I'm in love," announced Lucas.

"Oh great. And who is the victim?"

"I'm in love with this place. Have you ever seen anything more perfect?"

George looked round the terrace, saw the glow of the breaking waves, felt the sea breeze on his face and sniffed the *"gallo pinto"* being prepared in the kitchen.

"I guess not Lucas. But try and remember we're not here for vacation."

Lucas frowned. "You're right. But when our business is over I'm coming back. Right here to this hotel....."

"This shack," corrected George.

"Call it what you like. It's paradise man. And while we locate our little Kraut friend and lay a few plans for ambushing him I think we're going to do some intensive training. Too many Cuba Libres George, too many beers. I'm going to get fat again if I'm not careful and your going to lose your slender silhouette."

George waved at the barman. *"Dos platos de Gallo Pinto con huevos por favor. Y dos Cuba Libres mientras que estamos esperando."***

---

*   *Typical Costa Rican dish mixing beans with rice*

**   *"Two helpings of Gallo Pinto with eggs please. And two Cuba Libres while we are waiting."*

Lucas looked at him with raised eyebrows. "Are you manifesting defiance in the presence of your elder brother and life long mentor?"

"Yup. I take charge tonight. A couple of drinks, a good meal to soak them up and then we hit Tamarindo. I want another little fling. I'm developing a taste for Costa Rican nightlife. We deserve a bit of relaxation."

Lucas sighed. "You mean we haven't had enough for the last forty eight hours? Jesus, you're the one who was getting all sanctimonious about not being here for vacation."

"'Sanctimonious' like Saint Emilion?" Queried George.

****

Some six hours later and, having got hopelessly lost in the crisscrossing tracks between Tamarindo and Playa Grande, down to their last few drops of petrol, Lucas and George arrived back at El Bucanero.

George staggered tipsily into his room accompanied by a girl who called herself Rosa.

Lucas went for a drunken jog and a swim, watched the dawn breaking over the ocean and started thinking about Gerhardt Teuber.

Was it going to be as easy as it had been with Hans?

ALARM SYSTEMS

///

GERHARDT WAS AN EGOCENTRIC MAN, to the extent that he needed absolutely nobody else on the planet. He could survive happily on his own for the rest of his life. Unfortunately, he had discovered that even isolating himself at the end of the Playa Grande beach did not eradicate the occasional surfer or tourist or even inspector from the Costa Rican government's vast and highly dedicated Ministry of the Environment.

But he could watch them from a distance and they never really approached his house, which was sufficiently back from the waterfront and camouflaged behind coconut trees and tall pampas grass to be invisible.

There was something of the rodent about Gerhardt. He had highly developed survival instincts and had always prided himself on being able to sniff danger from a huge distance. And when he heard a knock on the door his whiskers twitched immediately.

He slipped silently into what he called his study and flipped a couple of switches to activate his CCTV system. The screen flickered and then cleared. It was the postman who came about once every three weeks with one or two of a small selection of bills he had to pay: local rates, mobile phone, a fixed telephone line which he only used for accessing the internet, and electricity (a flat rate as he had his own generator).

"Correo Senor. Soy Manuel."

Gerhardt frowned, he hated any disturbance, but he wanted to stay on good terms with the postman whom he tipped regularly; he had explained to him that his privacy was paramount and if Manuel would be his eyes and ears in Tamarindo and all along the Playa Grande then the tipping would continue.

---

*   *"Your post. It's Manuel."*

*"Hola Manuel, que hay de nuevo? No hay nada de interesante, nada que deberia saber?"**

Manuel spoke reasonable English and never let Gerhardt practise his Spanish.

"No sir, just the usual. Tourists, surfers everywhere."

"Good, that is what I want to hear." Gerhardt took the two envelopes which Manuel proffered and was already turning back to enter his house when Manuel spoke again.

"Only one thing which might interest you."

Gerhardt stopped in his tracks. He looked at Manuel with raised eyebrows.

"Couple of Britanicos staying at El Bucanero. They asked me how to get to your house. They had the address but as it's just the name of your house on Playa Grande they couldn't find it. They were really nice, spoke Spanish. They bought me a beer."

Gerhardt shook slightly. Nobody but nobody had his address except Hans. He tried to maintain a calm appearance.

"That's interesting. Maybe some old friends. Did you get their names?"

Manuel nodded. "Just their first names. Lucas and George."

Gerhardt gave him a lavish tip. "I know them well. They want to pay me a surprise visit. Fantastic. Manuel, promise me you won't tell them you told me. It will spoil their fun completely. I'm going to have to pretend I didn't know they were coming." He smiled conspiratorially and pressed a twenty dollar bill into his hand.

*"Por supuesto Senor,"*** replied Manuel.

Gerhardt watched him depart and walked quickly inside.

Lucas. There was only one Lucas he knew of and he was one of the last people on earth he wanted to see.

** *"Hi Manuel, what's up? Nothing of interest, nothing I should know about?"*

*** *"Of course Sir."*

He walked down to the shack where the girl lived. She was sweeping up and he felt the usual stirring as he saw her magnificent figure.

But today was different. The stirring abated as he snapped back to reality, survival mode. He noted her surprise and relief that he was not going to indulge in his usual fantasy, a sort of rape scene in which he tied her up and wilfully hurt her when he penetrated.

"Belinda."

"Yes sir?"

"I don't want you anywhere near the house for a few days. I will have some friends staying and I don't want any interruptions."

"Yes sir."

"In fact you may consider yourself free until Thursday. You can go and see your mother in San Jose if you want. If you leave you go via the beach, I don't want to see you leaving by the gate. When you come back, same thing."

"Yes sir." Belinda was used to Teuber's eccentricities and enigmatic demands but she was nevertheless curious about what lay behind this latest request.

She watched him return up the path to the main house and sat down to reflect on her options. It would be great to get out, have a change from this circumscribed existence. San Jose? Why not? Walk in the streets, buy some pretty clothes, spend some of the money she'd been saving. She'd been putting aside all her salary for months. By Costa Rican standards she was well off. She would buy presents.

She decided to wait until early evening and walk, via the beach as instructed, to the dusty road where a bus passed every hour on the way to Tamarindo. She would get another bus to Liberia and change again for San Jose. Travelling by night would be so much quicker.

She packed a small bag and gratefully stayed away from the house.

Gerhardt Teuber sat in his office, thinking hard while he cleaned and loaded his revolver.

Above all no panic. They were looking for him so either he ran for it or he killed them. Tried to kill them. If he ran they would probably catch up. After all, they'd tracked him down to the other side of the world. So he would have to stay. And he would have to devise a method of dealing with them which didn't jeopardise his own life. Some kind of trap. They might arrive at any time although logically he expected them after sunset.

He stared down the barrel of his gun and noticed that his hands were sweating. They were always humid and reptilian to touch, as Belinda knew to her cost. But now they were wet and slippery. A sure sign his nerves were on edge.

BREAK IN

LUCAS' PLAN HAD BEEN FORMULATED in a slightly cavalier fashion, but as he pointed out to George there was very little they could prepare. They couldn't anticipate Teuber's movements and they couldn't obtain more than a discreet preview of the outside of the house itself.

What they really couldn't foresee was how Gerhardt was going to react to a gun being held to his head. It had worked like a charm with Hans Teuber and he had been left with no options anyway because of the threat of disclosure of his collusion with a drug dealer and the subsequent embezzlement of the latter's ill-gotten gains.

"Early morning or late at night?" Lucas asked George

"Early morning."

"A dawn raid eh?"

"You got it," said George.

They were sitting on the terrace of "El Bucanero" watching, as had become their wont, the pelicans flying back home and the infinite variety of the waves.

Five days had gone by since their arrival in Tamarindo. Five days which Lucas used to jog and swim and practice his Krav Maga. After their first sortie into Tamarindo he had abstained from drink, cigarettes and the sultry charms of the local girls. George managed to moderate his consumption of the first two but claimed the girls were as good a way of getting fit as any other.

After meeting Manuel they had walked the three kilometres along the beach to Gerhardt Teuber's house, slipping into the forest a few hundred metres before arriving. It had been early evening when they set off and dusky when they got to their destination.

The house was perfectly visible provided they approached laterally from the forest. It was skilfully built out of wood. The roof overshot the walls by some two metres, obviously designed to provide ample shade to the first floor terraces which surrounded the house and which in turn would shade the ground floor ones. The wood appeared to be freshly treated and varnished leaving a slight tang in the air.

George had grabbed Lucas' arm when he saw Belinda walking up the path from her cabin at the bottom of the garden.

"For Christ's sake," Lucas whispered. "This is not the time. Concentrate."

"That's what I'm doing."

"Shut up and carry on filming."

They had seen Gerhardt coming out of the front door. He had passed by the girl without so much as turning his head and sat down with a beer at a table which stood near one of his beloved banana trees.

"Miserable looking sod," commented George.

Lucas nodded his head. "He's going to look a lot more miserable before long."

****

Two days later they left the Bucanero at 4.00a.m. George carried the unloaded revolver they had purchased in San Jose. The beach seemed slightly luminous, as did the ocean, both dimly lit by the moon. Their eyes soon adjusted.

They walked in silence for half an hour until they reached the dip in the forest where they had entered previously. Lucas led the way with a small torch. After another ten minutes of stealthy progress they found themselves at the top of the sandy hillock to the left of the villa which had provided such a good vantage point. There was total silence apart from the dull roar of the waves.

"This is creepy," said George.

"Bollocks."

They sat and watched the villa for a few minutes. The window on the left of the main entrance was open. There were no lights on apart from a lantern outside the front door giving out a dim yellow glow which barely extended beyond a couple of metres. They looked at each other.

"Looks like our friend is not worried about intruders," observed Lucas.

"Nobody worries about intruders here. People just surf."

"So what do we do? Break in or wait until the Kraut wakes up and comes out to inspect his banana trees?"

George thought for a minute. "We always said we would wait until he was outside. We don't know the inside of his house. The window is tempting but we'll make too much noise and he might escape."

"OK."

They settled back, somehow less confident. The seconds turned into minutes and the minutes into an hour. The sun was up and it was 6.30h when George nudged Lucas in the ribs.

They looked down towards the villa and saw Gerhardt walk out with a mug of coffee. He sat down. The brothers looked at each other, nodded and walked down towards Gerhardt with a smile on their faces.

Gerhardt smiled back. His revolver was tucked in the back of his khaki shorts. It was loaded, oiled and primed. When they were within five metres he snatched it out and, despite his rush of panic and adrenalin, pointed it steadily at them, holding it with both hands.

"Welcome to Costa Rica Lucas. And little brother George I presume? How nice to see you. Raise your hands and get down on your knees."

Lucas and George said nothing, did as they were told, numbed with astonishment. Gerhardt remained silent and then ordered them to stand up and walk ahead of him into the villa. He herded them inside, pointing an increasingly shaky revolver at them.

"One false move and I shoot," he said, biting his tongue at the clichéd words.

Lucas snorted scornfully. "Bullshit, you haven't got the guts......."

He didn't get any further. In panic mode Gerhardt pulled the trigger unintentionally and a bullet ripped across Lucas' shoulder causing him to scream. George instinctively stood between the two men and, hands raised even further, tried to calm Gerhardt down.

"Don't shoot again. Don't listen to Lucas. We'll do as you say."

Gerhardt stared in amazement at the wounded Lucas who was clutching his shoulder and wincing.

"Next time I aim for his head," he managed to say. "Open the door there, on your left, and both of you go inside. I'm going to have to think about what to do with you. And you're going to tell me what the fuck you're doing here."

Lucas did his best to smother the pain and shock and give Gerhardt a look of disdain and hatred, as he walked sullenly into the room. George followed. The door slammed shut and they heard the heavy bolt being drawn closed on the outside. They stood in the pitch dark for a minute.

"Are you OK ? Shit, you nearly got yourself killed you stupid bastard. Let me have a look."

Lucas shook his head. "It's nothing. A graze, that's all. You can't see anything anyway. Let's find a fucking light switch, if there is one."

George fumbled in his pockets for his lighter and they found a switch by the door.

They looked round the room in silence. Racks of wine and neat shelving with fruit, German sausage and cans of food. The room was small, some three metres by four and very cool. An air conditioning vent was apparent in the top of the wall above the wine racks and one light bulb shone from the ceiling.

"Well, looks like we're not going to get hungry," said George.

"Or thirsty. Look at these wines man. Same as mine, Margaux, Cheval Blanc, Saint Emilion.........Jesus, he's got that CUNE Rioja, 1970."

"CUNE?" Asked George. "Never heard of it. Find me something alliterative to describe its soul Lucas. Might ease the pain."

"Cunnilingual."

"Oh man. I have to admire you."

George paused. He looked at Lucas. "It was as if he was waiting for us."

"Yeah, well, I've worked that one out already. We gave our names to that Manuel guy, the postman. Just shows, one Cuba Libre too many and suddenly you throw caution to the winds and imagine everyone is your best friend."

"*We* throw caution to the winds."

They both pulled a crate of wine down from the shelves and sat down on their improvised seats in silence. George peered at Lucas' crate. Some kind of Burgandy. He looked at his watch. It was only 07.00h.

"I'd propose a thirsty firsty but it's bit early, even for you Lucas. Take your shirt off, you can have some brandy on your arm as consolation. I assume it acts as a disinfectant."

LOVING COUSINS

"HANS!"

"Gerhardt?" Hans Teuber's heart was undergoing some serious strain. First the Lucas debacle, then Krazicek, now the man he had betrayed. This was not a call he was looking forward to. He didn't like the tone of Gerhardt's voice. It was not the tone of a man suffering from the shock of physical attack and the loss of his life's savings.

"What the fuck is going on? How come you gave my address away? Why didn't you call me ....?" Gerhardt's voice was rising by the second.

Hans waited for him to stop. He gathered his wits.

"Gerhardt, are you OK? Did Lucas come to see you?"

"You know bloody well he came to see me. You gave him my address. Why? What are you trying to do to me?"

Hans took a deep breath. "Nothing, I swear it. Lucas beat me up and forced me to give him your address. And he said if I warned you he'd have me shot. He meant it. They want the money we took from the safe. Together with everything else. They made me transfer all of mine and they wanted to do the same thing to you. I swear to you, I had no option."

"You're despicable."

"What happened Gerhardt?"

Gerhardt paused. He'd known Hans all his life. He knew he wasn't lying. But he was still furious and indignant. At the same time he was also not a little proud of what he had accomplished and anxious to share it with his fat cousin.

"They found me and walked in at 6.30h in the morning."

Hans waited, breathless. On the one hand he wanted Gerhardt to have suffered the same humiliation as himself. On the other hand if by some miracle Gerhardt had escaped, which was apparently the case, then maybe this meant there was some way of salvaging his own situation. Then he thought about Krazicek and groaned inwardly. No one could escape from Krazicek.

"But I outwitted them," Gerhardt continued. "I could see there was something wrong the second I opened the door."

He decided to embellish his story.

"There was Lucas and his stupid brother standing there. I threw my coffee in Lucas' face and slammed the door, locked it and got my gun. That took me about three seconds 'cos I keep it in a drawer in the hall. Then I pulled the door open again and they were still there, Lucas was swearing and rubbing his eyes."

Hans Teuber rubbed his own eyes. *Gott im himmel.*

"You must be crazy. Lucas is dangerous."

"That's what I thought. That's why I acted so quickly."

"What happened next?"

Gerhardt was enjoying himself, Hans' gasping admiration was music to his ears.

"Easy. I locked them up and decided to call you."

"Locked them up?" Hans asked incredulously.

"I've got a room. A special room, not a cellar, but air conditioned where I keep my wine and stuff. A sort of larder I guess, no windows and a special door, really thick, made to keep the heat out and the cold in."

Hans giggled despite himself. "You've locked Lucas in a room where you stock your wine?"

"There's no corkscrew. And they should be freezing their arses off by now, I've put the temperature down to the minimum."

Hans needed time to think. All the parameters had changed. His Machiavellian brain was going into overdrive.

"Give me half an hour Gerhardt. I'll call you back."

BACK HOME

NATHALIE LISTENED TO CHLOE with a small frown on her face. It was no later than 7.00h.

"It's not normal Nath. Lucas always calls me every day and I call him. I haven't heard from him for two days now and he doesn't pick up. Has George called you?"

Nathalie tried to remember the last time she had spoken to George. Their estrangement was deepening by some strange telepathic force, as if their mutual infidelity had been tacitly understood.

"We don't speak nearly as often as you and Lucas. I haven't talked to him for about four days. But that doesn't worry me. Shall I try him now and call you back? Maybe Lucas' mobile has broken down. Maybe there's no network. Costa Rica is mainly jungle as far as I know."

Chloe was clearly choking back her tears.

"He would have called anyway. He would have used George's 'phone or called from his hotel. Something has happened."

Nathalie felt a little stab of panic. She was definitely out of love with George but that didn't mean she was totally indifferent to his welfare. And then her plans with Krazicek were at stake.

"Two days is not a long time Chloe, don't worry. But I'll try and call George anyway."

She put the telephone down and walked slowly to her room and flopped onto her bed. It was still early in the morning and the Niçois sun, pink and round as a grapefruit, was casting its soft light on the eastern side of Mont Boron.

Krazicek was in his hotel, they had decided to have a one night break and catch up on some sleep.

She tried to calculate the time difference. Costa Rica had to be at least six hours behind. She picked up her mobile and called George. His polite voice on the answering machine requested her to leave a message. She asked him to call as soon as possible.

She got up again and went through to the kitchen/bar which had been designed by Lucas when he lived there. Of course. Any liveable space in Lucas' environment had to be geared to drinking. She made a coffee and lit an unusually early cigarette.

She thought about Lucas for a minute. They had never really hit it off. Lucas had looked at her with his blue eyes and apparently dismissed her as of no interest. There was a definite lack of trust also. If her plans with Krazicek worked out his distrust would be justified. A hundred fold.

She sent a text message to George: *please call me any time asap.*

****

Krazicek was awake too. He'd received, much to his annoyance, a call at midnight. He was tired and needed an undisturbed night. When he saw Hans Teuber's number he was instantly curious. The guy was so terrified of him he would only call if it was important.

"What's up Teuber? Why are you calling so late?"

"I am very sorry. It is very important."

"Tell me then."

"I got a call from Gerhardt!" Hans Teuber sounded scared. How was this crazy bastard going to react?

"So?"

"It's barely credible. Lucas went to pay him a visit as expected. Gerhardt somehow got the better of him, and his brother, and locked them up in his house. They're prisoners!"

"What?"

"I'm serious. Gerhardt sounds very pissed off. He has a gun, he sounds as if he's going to shoot them. What do we do? I have to call him back in half an hour. He knows they stole my money and that they were planning to take his too. I had to tell him. As soon as he saw Lucas he must have guessed it was to do with the money anyway."

Krazicek rubbed his jaw and thought for a minute. They could lose everything. And then he saw things more simply.

"Call him back and tell him to wait a couple of days. Tell him not to kill them yet."

"Why? I mean how can I convince him?"

"Tell him whatever you like Teuber, I'm going out there to sort out this mess. It may just make things go quicker when you think about it. Instead of all that pussy footing around trying to get the digipass and the code I'll just break everybody's arse and get the transfers done my way."

Hans Teuber swallowed. He knew what getting things done *à la Krazicek* involved.

"I will do as you say."

"Good boy, Teuber. Every time you do me a good turn makes it less likely that you suffer a horrible death. But the dogs are still there Teuber, so don't get clever."

Hans Teuber swallowed again and spoke with his thick German accent.

"I swear to you, I will not get clever."

Krazicek put the telephone down, opened his laptop and then checked on flights to Madrid. He was bound to get a direct connection to San Jose with Iberia. A flight from Nice to Madrid was leaving at 9.30h in the morning. The Iberia connection left Madrid at 12.00h. Perfect. He could even get a few hours sleep.

TIME TO REFLECT

LUCAS SAT UNCOMFORTABLY in his miniature prison and reflected on his plight. Who would find him here, locked inside a bungalow on the edge of the pacific, miles from even the smallest village? Maybe he was going to die here. Maybe a pile of bones would be discovered at some future date. His bones, but no one would bother with a DNA test and even if they did they wouldn't identify Lucas Watt, private banker from the South of France.

And what about George? Shit, he was the one who had got his younger brother into this mess.

He pulled out the few sheets of paper he had found, the stub of a pencil and started writing.

There are supposedly six billion people on this planet and probably the same number, maybe twice, in the whole history of the world that is, who have passed away. Where they have gone, if anywhere, will never be known. Where we, the ones who are still alive, will go when our turn comes will never be known either. The closest you can get to some tangible idea of life after death is through your children as a genetic continuation of yourself. The idea of some recycling process as your body is reintegrated into the ecological chain seems true but inadequate from a spiritual point of view! I was watching Euronews not long ago (in Spanish of course, got to keep it going) and there was an advertisement for "Malaysia, always Asia". What attracted my attention was the content and text of the advertisement which showed images of a perfect couple, young, beautiful, in love, wreathed in smiles etc., performing various activities- climbing mountains, chasing exotic butterflies, canoeing along rivers, watching glorious sunsets- in the "thirty million year old rain forests".

Well, thirty million years is as close as you can get to eternity I reckon, so if the Malaysian rain forest can do it through constant reseeding of itself why not us, the Watt clan, who presumably crawled out of the primeval swamps in some appalling shape or form at about the same time?

"One life". I think that is a good title for anyone seeking to transmit a few antecedents to his children. One life because there are so many other people's lives that you have to stay humble; one life because for better or for worse every life is unique; one life because you only have one life (so enjoy it and travel from A to Z as best you can without screwing up too much); one life because maybe, coming back to that elusive notion of eternity, it's meaningful to contemplate that rain forest which has been around so long and, global warming permitting, will still be there when what is left of me is you...........and yours.

"What are you doing Lucas? Writing a fucking novel?"

Lucas sighed and tore up the piece of paper. He suddenly felt ashamed. It was as if he had been writing his own epitaph. There was a melancholic, even valedictory undertone to his scribbling which made him squirm. Thank God George hadn't seen it.

"Someone else has been putting pen to paper. Look."

A piece of paper slid under the door. George picked it up and read out the message which had been scrawled in pencil:

I know why you are here, Hans told me despite your threats. You have zero options. You will stay in this room until you return Hans' funds. To my account of course. If you refuse for too long you will die. There will be two toilet breaks a day. I do not want you animals soiling my house.

"Fucking Kraut bastard," said Lucas.

"Fucking clever Kraut bastard if you ask me," replied George. "He's right, we have no options. But if, or rather when, we send the money, what happens to us? That's what I want to know."

"He doesn't know, otherwise he would have told us. He hasn't figured any alternative to killing us."

"Maybe that's about our only chance."

"What do you mean?" Lucas looked up.

"Well, as long as he knows we think we're going to be shot whether we hand over the money or not he also knows he's going to have to negotiate if he wants to get it. Otherwise we may as well drink ourselves to death in here. Better than a bullet in the head."

Lucas stood up and stretched.

"He's been a step ahead of us up until now. But you may be right. We'd better start thinking about what we can offer. How can we guarantee we're not going to come back, after we've signed over the money, and stick a gun up his arse?"

TAMARINDO ARRIVALS

KRAZICEK LOST NO TIME in getting to San Jose. He arrived at 16.00h local time, barely twenty four hours after Hans Teuber's telephone call.

Once in the centre, a few discreet questions to the cab driver accompanied by a large tip procured him a small revolver. From there he had taken the same cab back to the airport and caught a flight to Tamarindo where he checked in at the Hyatt. He had quickly located the whereabouts of Gerhardt Teuber's villa.

It was 21.00h by now and he felt good.

He showered and changed into black trousers and tee-shirt, a pair of strong rubber soled shoes and a cotton jacket. He checked his revolver and strapped it together with his hunting knife to his leg. Vuk had always done that. By 21.30h he was in a taxi that took him to Playa Grande.

"You come to watch the giant turtles Senor?" asked the driver.

"Yeah. Just drop me as far down the beach as you can get. I'm going to spend the night waiting for them."

The taxi stopped when the track became too rough. Krazicek paid and waited until the taillights had disappeared before starting a light jog. Within fifteen minutes he felt nicely warmed up and he recognized the curve in the shoreline which he had been told indicated the area of Gerhardt Teuber's house.

He decided to enter the garden directly from the beach and skirted round Belinda's humble annexe until he could see the main house. The moon provided more than enough light and he had no need to use his torch.

No dogs. Amazing. He looked for signs of alarm systems and could find none. He followed the path up the side of the garden, past the banana trees and reached the side of the house. The Pacific roared in the background and he could make out the light at Gerhardt Teuber's front door.

Gerhardt was in his office, plainly visible through the window. He seemed to be in a good mood because every couple of minutes he rose from his chair and performed a small dance, clapping his hands together and smiling up at the ceiling. Krazicek could see his revolver on the desk, next to a half finished bottle of whisky. Great, the fat bastard was drunk. Obviously celebrating something.

Krazicek looked around and saw Gerhardt's garden table. It was a heavy object made of some kind of thick exotic wood and measured some four feet square. He lifted it and grunted his approval. All of thirty kilos. He turned it upside down and charged directly at the window.

If Gerhardt Teuber had been prone to heart attacks like his cousin he would certainly have had one. The shattering glass followed by the table itself landing on the floor in front of him combined to make a deafeningly explosive noise and Krazicek, hurling himself through the window frame as he screamed obscenities in Serbian, magnified the noise and the shock.

Gerhardt sagged back against his desk with his mouth gaping and his heart pounding well above the maximum allowed for a sixty five year old man in his condition. Krazicek whipped the revolver off the desk and punched him hard on the chin. Gerhardt went down like a puppet which had suddenly lost its strings and lay unconscious on the floor.

Krazicek ripped one of the lamps off the desk and tied his victim tightly to the desk leg with the electric cable. He picked up the whisky bottle, saw the "Famous Grouse" label and took a swig. The remainder he poured on top of the unfortunate Gerhardt.

No reaction. Shit, he hoped he hadn't hit him too hard. He slapped him, still no reaction. He saw a full bottle of soda water on a shelf and emptied it directly on Gerhardt's face. There was a groan and Gerhardt started blowing bubbles out of his mouth.

"Wakey, wakey. Time to start talking to your new friend."

Gerhardt heard the words through a mist of pain and his head was spinning so much he couldn't open his eyes. The only thing he could remember he didn't want to remember. It was the nightmarish vision of a huge man coming through the window with the obvious intention of murdering him. He started passing out again but received such a painful kick that he snapped back to reality.

And the reality was not good.

"Hans?" He said feebly.

"Yeah, Hans. He gave me your address. Told me you'd been a naughty boy. Gone and locked up his best friends."

"His best friends?" Said Gerhardt stupidly.

"Lucas and George. You've got them locked away somewhere. I want to know where and I want to know what you've agreed with them. What has happened to Hans' money?"

Gerhardt Teuber maintained a numbed silence. This was too much for him to digest. Krazicek decided to apply some additional shock treatment. He pulled out his knife and plunged the blade a couple of centimetres into Gerhardt's thigh. As the high-pitched screams reached a climax he pulled the knife out and stabbed the other thigh.

Krazicek left him on his own to find the kitchen, brought back a full plastic basin of cold water and hurled it into his victim's face. Gerhardt Teuber stopped screaming and proceeded to blow bubbles again, this time red ones out of his nose. As he became aware of the pain he started whimpering.

"I'll ask you one more time. Where is Hans' money?"

"I haven't got it. Lucas has got it. He hasn't agreed to transfer it to my account yet." Gerhardt moaned and tried ineffectually to wipe the snot from his nose by lifting his shoulder. He stared helplessly at his legs which were oozing blood.

"So where is Lucas and where is his brother? Where the fuck are they?"

Gerhardt squirmed feebly on the floor and pointed vaguely in the direction of the door with his head. "In the store room."

"Store room?"

"The place I store my food. And my wine."

Krazicek snorted. "Wine? From what I've heard about Lucas there's going to be fuck all left of that. Where's the key?"

"There is no key. Just a bolt on the outside. A big bolt."

Krazicek started to wipe the knife on Gerhardt's shirtfront.

"How long have they been in there?"

"Two days."

"It's going to smell pretty bad in there."

"I let them go to the bathroom twice a day. I've told them I'm going to shoot them if they don't release the funds. They just insult me and say 'No you won't, no you won't.'"

"Stalemate huh?"

"Not totally. I told them I was in no hurry, that they could spend the rest of their lives in the storeroom as far as I was concerned. That stopped them in their tracks. They're obviously thinking about things differently. Claustrophobia and cold will get them in the end......"

Teuber's head nodded and he passed out again.

Krazicek looked at him with alarm. The stupid bastard looked as if he was going to die. Better get his transfer sorted out first. He fetched more water and a couple of kitchen towels which he bound around the two wounds. Then he poured some more water on his face and pulled him into a sitting position. Teuber woke up and stared in mute misery at his tormentor.

"I'm going to make things very simple for you. You have one chance of staying alive. I know you've got exactly the same amount of money as your partner Hans."

He broke off with a laugh.

"Exactly the same as Hans *used* to have. Anyway, thirty million dollars has to go into my account and you keep any surplus that's left. You'll be able to live here just like before and you'll be free. I sort out Lucas and get rid of him and his brother. Then I say goodbye."

Teuber made to speak but was cut short.

"Don't ask for any guarantees. Just reassure yourself with the fact that I couldn't give a fuck whether you live or die. It's your only chance Gerhardt Teuber. Yes or no?" Krazicek looked meaningfully at the knife.

"Yes."

"Good, let's get to work. Fax machine, telephone, computer, whatever you need to send the instructions."

He heaved Teuber to his feet. Teuber screamed again. Krazicek laughed.

******

Teuber typed out his instructions to his three banks. Twenty million dollars would leave Andorra and five million dollars from each of his banks in San Jose. It was exactly midnight. Krazicek watched him with glowing eyes.

"Just a few hours now," said Krazicek.

"Why, to what?"

"To when you call your banks to confirm the instructions. Andorra will be waking up around 3.00h our time. Then you go to sleep until 9.00h and we call San Jose."

"And then?"

"Then we'll see."

Gerhardt Teuber sat down miserably on the floor as Krazicek practiced throwing his knife at the thick wooden door.

The repetitive action helped him to think. He relished two things. One was Lucas' reaction when he saw him. He was going to see the ghost of Vuk and that was going to be hilarious. And then he wanted to tell George about Nathalie.

But before that was the question of the money. Between Teuber and Lucas there would be another sixty million dollars in his account. That was bigger than any individual commission from any arms deal he had brokered for Sadaam Hussein. He would have a total balance of one hundred and forty five million dollars in the bank. Shit, too much for any one bank. He would contact his friendly Swiss banker, Jacques Pelletier, and get his fortune spread across a few more institutions.

And then he would really start sowing havoc.

And there was one more priority, in fact the priority *par excellence*: Amra. He was going to get that bitch, that cold-blooded whore. And she was going to suffer. This time she was going to be the prey, the one who was being tracked. He'd shared women with Vuk in the past, but not this way.

DÉJÀ VU

GERHARDT TEUBER was barely functioning. His life had turned into a nightmare and all he wanted was to survive. Let anything happen, let the crazy fucking bastard who was torturing and robbing him have everything. Even his clothes. But please God, let him free, let him live. He'd be happy to walk stark naked down the Fürst-Franz-Josef-Strasse in Vaduz just to stay alive. Please God.

He had listened to the telephone ringing on the other side of the Atlantic. He had explained to the Bank of Andorra that the money would leave temporarily to complete a deal, that it would be coming back, that it was just a loan to a certain "Fairtrade Corporation". He also explained that in fact much more would come back in six months as he reaped his profits. His relationship manager at the bank was disappointed by the exit of such a substantial sum but reassured by the promise of its return together with additional funds at a later date.

Six hours later he had done the same with his banks in San Jose. He was now thirty million poorer and didn't even know if he was going to stay alive.

The maniacal brute sprawled across his sofa was snoring. Jesus, he was a big bastard. Gerhardt watched Krazicek's wrestler chest heaving peacefully and felt weak and humiliated.

His sniffling woke up Krazicek who uncoiled in a second. It was 10.30h. He had slept one hour but he felt fine.

****

"The gun is unloaded. Just point it as usual when you let them out for their morning ablutions. Then you put them back in the storeroom and I take over. Got it?"

Gerhardt Teuber nodded his head in dejected acquiescence and took the gun. It was his and he could feel how much lighter it was with no ammunition. Krazicek hid behind the door of the study to listen and observe. He was bursting with curiosity to see Lucas, the man who had played such a central role in the last chapter of Vuk's life. And George, the man he had so thoroughly cuckolded and Amra's one time lover.

Teuber slid back the bolt on the door and stepped back quickly. Lucas pulled the door back violently and swore at him.

"You bastard. What's this then, torture by not letting us go to the toilet? What the fuck are you playing at? And what the fuck has happened to your face? Jesus, your legs! You fall out of the upstairs window or something?"

"Just go and do your needs and get back in your cage. One by one. Looks like you're the most desperate so your brother stays until you come back. And don't take all morning."

Weirdly, Krazicek's presence boosted Gerhardt's confidence.

"Afternoon," replied Lucas petulantly.

He disappeared into the bathroom and slammed the door. Teuber bolted the storeroom door again. The sound of the shower just filtered through to the corridor.

After ten minutes Lucas emerged, his wet hair swept back and his face fresh from a shave. Teuber waved the revolver at him indicating he should open the storeroom again. Lucas obeyed, scowling, and waited for George to come out and take his turn.

"OK Lucas, feel better?"

"Yeah, thanks. Thought I was going to explode. See you in a minute."

Lucas walked into his miniature prison and stared defiantly at Gerhardt Teuber as he closed the door again.

Krazicek reflected for a moment and decided the moment had come to confront Lucas. Much better if George wasn't there. He waved Teuber back into his office, tied him with the same cable to the same table leg and put his finger against his lips.

"One squeak and you die."

Gerhardt nodded, staring with wide pleading eyes at the nightmarish giant. Krazicek bared his teeth and walked quickly to the storeroom. He slid back the bolt quietly and pushed open the door.

Lucas looked up.

His mouth opened and he started gagging for air. His head started spinning and his heart lurched violently. A perfect image of Vuk's corpse, riddled with bullets from the remorseless Amra, swept before him. He tried to scream but there was no air in his lungs, he felt himself collapsing, the room turning on its axis as he clutched automatically at the nearest object. He felt an agonising rush of blood to his chest and his head.

The crate of 1970 CUNE Rioja crashed to the floor with Lucas on top of it. Krazicek studied him. He couldn't have hoped for a better reaction. Maybe he'd had a heart attack?

He slipped quickly out of the storeroom locking the door and walked down the corridor to the bathroom which had been locked from the outside. He waited for George to signal he had finished. He unlocked the door, took a step back and greeted George with a deadpan look and his knife held casually in his right hand.

George didn't quite register the face, all he knew was that his throat was about to be slit open. He reeled backwards and tried to slam the bathroom door. Krazicek gave it a mighty kick which took it off its hinges and sent George flying back against the wall.

"Come out slowly and you won't get hurt. Take a good look at me and tell me if you recognize me."

George staggered cautiously out to the corridor and raised his eyes. In the same instant he recognized Vuk and felt the blood freeze in his veins. He stared with horrified fascination at the resurrection of the man who had been dead seven years.

"Long time no see George."

George backed away again, pure animal terror making his body go numb. There was silence for a full minute.

"OK, the joke's over George. I'm not Vuk. You should know that, don't tell me you never googled him, never found out he had a twin brother."

George's nervous system started to slowly function again as his brain dealt with the fact that this was not a ghost. He should have remembered: Krazicek, the identical twin. Shit, if he was as psychopathic as Vuk then he and Lucas might just as well commit suicide.

"You've come to avenge your brother." A rhetorical question. "Why here, why not Nice? Why now? How did you track us down to Tamarindo?"

"That's a lot of stupid questions in one go."

George suddenly frowned, hit by a fresh wave of panic. "Where's Lucas?"

"Last time I saw him he was crashed out on a crate of wine. Quite appropriate from what I've heard about him."

George started forward, only to find Krazicek's hideous hunting knife a millimetre from his throat. A huge rough hand pushed him back towards the wall.

"He'll live. I think."

"What?"

"He had a million volt shock when he saw me.....Lucas Watt had a million volt shock..... I hadn't thought of that. It was fascinating to watch. He really thought I was Vuk. He had a sort of convulsion and collapsed......."

"I have to see him," George shouted hysterically.

"If you're a good boy you will. The sooner you help me the sooner you get to help your brother. If you don't help me then you don't get to help him. And believe me, he needs help. I think he had a heart attack, just seeing me. I'm not kidding George."

"Help? What the fuck are you talking about? How can I help you?" George was lost in a sea of panic and confusion. He had to get to Lucas.

Krazicek's deadpan demeanor began to melt. He seemed angry all of a sudden.

"I've been to see Hans."

George was not even surprised. If this maniac could track him and Lucas to Tamarindo he could have found Hans without even breaking a sweat.

Krazicek continued: "So now you know how you can help. I'm going to make it easy for you. You speak to Jérôme, you get him to press the right buttons on the digipass, fax the bank, do whatever the fuck he has to and send the money to my company account. Then you can help Lucas."

George stared at him with bewilderment. "How do you know all this stuff?"

Krazicek shrugged enigmatically.

George started churning the options over in his mind. There weren't any.

"And then you shoot us? Great. That doesn't make a deal."

"Let me tell you something. Two things. First of all I can't think of any reason to shoot you. You're both so pathetic. You'll never find me anyway, nor the money which, incidentally, is almost exactly twice what you stole from Vuk. As soon as it hits that account it's going to be divided up in little bundles and scattered across five continents, a dozen offshore companies and trusts and as many banks. You little men are going to be so happy to get back to your mediocre lives you're going to try and forget me."

George tried to think clearly. He failed.

"What's the second thing?"

"My real punishment for you. Your total defeat, your humiliation. You're going to have to live with that for the rest of your lives."

George considered this. Where was the humiliation in being beaten by an experienced and ruthless crook? The defeat might be total but it was not a bitter pill to swallow in exchange for staying alive.

"Plus the fact that I will always have tabs on you. You step out of line and one of Lucas' children disappears. Lucas steps out of line and you suddenly lose an arm or a leg. Or your girlfriend. Not nice George. Your lives have changed for the worse. Permanently. But you stay alive."

George stared at him in silence. So much hatred. And all because of Vuk. The money wasn't the issue.

It was 11.00h local time, 17.00h in Nice. That meant Jérôme would almost certainly still be in the office in Nice. George had one priority in his mind. Get to Lucas. The loss of the money was meaningless compared to his brother's life.

They went through to Gerhardt's office. Gerhardt was dozing, exhausted on the floor, his hands still tied painfully to the table. Krazicek pointed at the telephone, his eyebrows raised mockingly.

"You get the transfer underway and ask for immediate value. A copy of the SWIFT transfer instruction must be sent to Jacques Pelletier, that's *jpelletier@unsb.ch*. You tell Jérôme to ask Pelletier to confirm back to you on your personal email the second the transaction has gone through."

George nodded and picked up the telephone.

As soon as Jérôme heard George's voice he knew something was wrong.

"George, everyone has been worrying about you; I've had Chloe and Nath on the line every two minutes. Why haven't you called sooner?"

George looked briefly at Krazicek. If Jérôme knew the situation he'd blow a fuse.

"There have been one or two developments. Unexpected ones. We got robbed, lost our mobiles, money, passports, you name it. But we're OK. Shit, I'm sorry to have got everyone upset like that. Call them, Chloe and Nath, and tell them everything is fine and we'll be able to call and talk........." George raised his eyebrows in Krazicek's direction. Krazicek made a rolling gesture with his finger.

"......Tomorrow. We're sorting out shit with the consulate, police, you name it. Anyway, Lucas lost his digipass also...."

"He did what? He took his digipass to Costa Rica? What the fuck for?"

Good. It was working. "Yeah, no comment. But even if the risks are virtually zero without the code it's a security breach and we've decided to move the money to another account. Immediately."

"What other account?"

"Lucas had this little offshore company account in Switzerland with UNSB. The guy who handles the account is called Jacques Pelletier. He's one of the senior guys, can get anything authorized and he'll be prepared to believe anything to get thirty million dollars into the bank. So Lucas has fed him some crap about the origin of funds and he's waiting for the them to arrive."

George could almost see Jérôme scratching his head.

"Are you sure?"

"Well, I'm just the messenger Jérôme. I don't understand banking stuff. All I know is that Lucas has made up his mind so I guess it's got to be done. In fact I know it's got to be done, I've never seen Lucas so insistent. He'll call you tomorrow; he's with the British consul right now. I'll wait for the confirmation from Pelletier but scan me a copy of the SWIFT transfer in the meantime. Make the old man happy."

Jérôme noted down account and email details and, slightly doubtfully, said he would get things done before going home.

George put the telephone down. Krazicek nodded approval.

"Good boy George. Good performance. You ever considered taking up acting?"

"I must see Lucas now."

Krazicek stared at him in silence for a full ten seconds. He nodded again and jerked his head in the direction of the store room.

"OK. Leave your email open before you go. I want to monitor those confirmations."

TRACKING

////

BRADEN LOOKED AT HIS WATCH. 08.00h in the CIA Headquarters at Langley. The surveillance and communication systems had highlighted the thirty million dollar transfer from Hans Teuber's account to an offshore company called Hornet Investments. This had stirred interest, the more so when the beneficiary bank in Cyprus had been forced to point to a corporate services provider called Charles Farrugia. And Farrugia had quickly agreed to give away the names of the ultimate beneficial owners : Lucas and George Watt and Jérôme Saiman.

It was amazing when he thought about it. Lucas Watt had been on the radar ever since the CIA had sniffed a connection with Vuk Racik's assassination. Vuk's death had put an end to what might have been a very expensive and time-consuming hunt for concrete proof of his war crimes and connections to narcotics and arms trading.

So Lucas, if it was indeed he who had pulled the trigger (more than once judging by the bullet ridden corpse), had unwittingly done a good turn to the CIA who were relieved and grateful that Vuk should be dealt such summary justice. They simply did not care about a few million dollars which probably ended up in Lucas' pocket.

Braden sighed. Imagine what it would have cost to take Vuk through the Hague and the legal imbroglio of international law. Which incidentally, and bizarrely, seemed to be useless at protecting those in need and highly effective in providing an infinite array of rights and escape routes to the real villains.

But what the hell was the trio up to now? They were in receipt of a serious amount of money emanating from Hans Teuber who was also on their surveillance list. This put them in another league and seemed incongruous. They'd been vetted several times and had never been judged capable of or likely to become players in big time money laundering. Weird.

And what the fuck were they doing in Costa Rica? Maybe they had just gone to have some fun and celebrate their recently acquired wealth.

Braden's team were also investigating, but without any immediate connection to anything in particular, Krazicek's disappearance from Baghdad. They had scrolled through the possibilities: Krazicek just bolting because of the two agents he'd found in his room? Or maybe he had been on his way out anyway because post 9/11 nobody stayed in Iraq if they could get out; or was he already worried about the arms dealing trail leading straight to his abode at the Baghdad Hilton; had he just been quite simply intending to retire to live peacefully off his ill-gotten gains? Where would he go?

It was Braden who made the hypothetical connection to Lucas because Lucas was on his mind after the transfer from Teuber. He got the report from Langley that the only person leaving Baghdad at the same time as Krazicek's disappearance was someone who had never officially entered Iraq. A certain Jon Vanhouteghem. And the latter showed up subsequently at one hotel in Madrid, two hotels in Monaco and one in Nice. What if Krazicek was at last picking up the scent and seeking to wreak revenge on the supposed killer of his brother and recoup some of Vuk's money? Lucas was going to be in serious danger. Did that really matter?

Braden's secretary walked in with coffee and a fresh list of red alerts. He thanked her, sipped the coffee and started his ritual of studying the lists.

"There are some new transfers that have been highlighted apart from the one for thirty million dollars. There is another for twenty million and two more for five million. All for the same beneficiary, same bank. Fairtrade Corporation, UNSB.

"Otherwise nothing special to report," she said coyly.

"Thanks. I'll have a look." Braden found himself watching her as she turned and left. Actually, she was very attractive. Would he do anything about it? That was the question.

She turned round at the door and the profile was good too. She looked pleased with herself and carried a cute little smirk.

"One thing you're going to love. Two of the transfers left from Costa Rica!"

Braden remained silent for a few seconds. Then he smiled at her.

"You certainly know how to get me excited."

They stared at each other, momentarily embarrassed by the ambiguity of his comment. Then they laughed. Some obscure barrier had been broken down.

She left the room and he studied the list of transfers. The one leaving Andorra made him frown. He hated Andorra for some reason. Something sordid about the place. Then his frown deepened. The two transfers from Costa Rica. Life was full of coincidences and in his trade they were what he looked for most. He loved it. Disparate bits of information, movements, people, all potentially connected. Hornet Investments made things even more intriguing. The real fun was just beginning.

He picked up the telephone and spoke to agent Newman, the man his secretary had once disparagingly described as 'tall, dark and not very handsome'. He had never lived down his christian name, foisted upon him by an adoring mother.

"Time to start pushing a few buttons Paul. We're onto something. Whether or not we've found the sixth circle I don't know but we just might be getting warm. Get the details of the account from my secretary and activate the contacts in the MROS. Get it blocked and every credit and debit traced since it was opened."

The MROS, or Money Laundering Reporting Office Switzerland, was the Swiss financial intelligence unit which functioned as a relay and filtration point between financial intermediaries and the law enforcement agencies. Emanating from the 1997 Money Laundering Act it was Braden's chosen entry point into the complex world of Swiss financial supervision and investigation, providing as it did an interface with the prosecuting authorities and a direct link to the Federal Office of Police.

"I'm on the way." Paul Newman was excited too.

DELERIUM

///

GEORGE STUMBLED INTO THE STOREROOM, helped by a violent push in the back from Krazicek before the door slammed shut. The light was on and Lucas was slumped in the corner. George had never seen him like that. He looked as if he had escaped from a lunatic asylum, white and shaking, mumbling incoherently.

"Lucas, for Christ's sake, it wasn't Vuk. Look me in the eyes. You remember he had a twin brother? Of course you do. Vuk's dead and buried. That was his fucking twin, he wanted to spook you. Lucas, can you hear me, do you understand?"

Lucas did not raise his head, he continued mumbling. George became seriously alarmed. The shock had apparently been too great for him.

"Speak to me, damn it, look at me Lucas."

Lucas raised his head slightly, not enough to look George in the eyes.

"It was him George. I swear to you. I'd recognize him anywhere, I've been having nightmares about him for long enough. That was him."

George decided to reduce the pressure. "OK Lucas, so that corpse we left on the Grande Corniche, riddled with bullets of which one was in the middle of its forehead, was not really dead?"

"No, he wasn't normal. He could have lived."

"Sorry Lucas, that's crap. Don't you remember? Even the police reports in the local newspaper confirmed he was dead, together with his foul little friend Tomas."

"It was him." Lucas raised his eyes and George recoiled slightly. Lucas looked ten years older and his expression was one of profound sadness.

George stood up, gave Lucas a reassuring smile and reached above him to a shelf with a variety of cognacs and rums. He chose a 'Duque de Alba', a Spanish brandy and the only one he recognized. As he did so his mind generated a satellite image, a zoom on Peniscola in Cataluna where he had last tasted 'Duque de Alba', followed by a zoom on Tamarindo and their bizarre prison.

He pulled the cork out and took a quick swig for himself as if to give an example to Lucas. He wiped his mouth.

"That's better, 'Duque de Alba' Lucas. Christ it tastes good." He offered the bottle to Lucas who took it hesitantly and then tipped his head back. He spluttered and swore.

"That's my boy, have some more."

Lucas took a second longer swig and appeared to relax a bit.

"Can I have a cigarette?"

"You can have anything you want, you can have a fucking joint if you want, just blow the smoke at the extractor up there or we'll both get asphyxiated." George kept his voice light and jocular. Everything normal.

"You wouldn't lie to me would you?"

"What would I do that for Lucas? Come on, give me the bottle. I'm going to have a ciggy too."

"It was like meeting the devil."

"He scared the shit out of me," said George, nudging Lucas' damaged nervous system back to some kind of equilibrium. "But he came clean straight away. He told me the truth. His name is Krazicek, he's a big mean bastard but I don't think he's got that killer look in his eyes. Not like Vuk. This guy ain't a softy, no way, but he ain't a psychopath either."

Lucas managed a bashful grin. "I'm sorry."

"Forget about it, the bastard stage-managed his appearance, anyone would have psyched out."

"But I'm still a fucking idiot."

"Agreed. So what's new?"

"I feel embarrassed." Lucas scratched his head and looked at the floor.

"Join the club mate, I think I pissed on myself. I thought he was going to kill me. Fucking great hunting knife stuck against my throat. Which reminds me......" George paused as he concentrated.

"What?"

"Good news and bad news; I'll give you the good news first. He's not going to kill us."

"Why not?"

"Weird. Something to do with humiliating us. A sort of punishment, with him as the Sword of Damocles hanging over our heads."

"Very weird," agreed Lucas, beginning to shed a few years and generally perk up. "But good news it is and that's putting it mildly. What's the other bit, the bad bit?"

"Guess."

The colour started draining out of Lucas' face again. "Oh no!" He paused as he watched his brother nodding his head. "And he's going to get Gerhardt's money too. He's taken over everything we set out to achieve."

"He's not *going* to get it Lucas, he's got it already. The only thing we can do now is wait to see how the bastard deals with us. And with Gerhardt Teuber for that matter. He looks really bad. He's bleeding from his legs. We got off lightly."

Lucas stared stupidly at the bottle of brandy and picked it up again. Then he started laughing.

George observed him. Good, the therapy was working.

CLEARING UP

%

KRAZICEK STARED AT THE CHAOS which surrounded him. He grinned. What a mess. Gerhardt Teuber was apparently fast asleep on the floor, there were shards of broken glass everywhere and bloodstains on the upturned furniture.

He contemplated his success. Sixty million dollars of fresh funds in his account. Add that to his existing assets and he was now seriously rich. He wished he could simply kill all three of his victims. Vuk wouldn't have thought twice about it but he wasn't Vuk. He didn't mind roughing people up, as the Teubers had found to their cost but he couldn't quite bring himself to commit cold-blooded murder.

He'd have to find a way to delay them, keep them prisoner for sufficient time to allow him to get back to Europe, sort out his finances with Pelletier in Geneva and then......then what?

Nathalie was the girl he wanted. He'd thought about it a lot. He would 'elope' with her as Teuber had suggested. Just hearing the old fashioned word in his head made him laugh.

He picked up the telephone and dialled her number. It would be about 21.00h in France. He wondered how long it would take for the connection to cross Costa Rica, the Atlantic and zip along the Mediterranean. Exactly two seconds.

"Hallo, Nathalie à l'appareil."

"Nathalie? It's me. How are you?"

"Krazicek! Where are you? I thought you'd forgotten all about me. I've never been so frustrated in all my life."

Krazicek laughed. "Cool it baby, cool it. I had to take a break, I was exhausted. You've been treating me like a sex toy."

Nathalie giggled, bubbling with excitement. "You haven't seen anything yet you poor man. When are you coming to take me back to bed?"

"Very soon. Listen, I want you to move out of your apartment tomorrow. Pack your stuff, store whatever you have to and go to

Paris. Get the best room at the George V and enjoy yourself. I'll be with you in a couple of days."

"Do you mean it Krazicek? What are you saying? Is this a naughty weekend?"

"Certainly that, could be quite a long one."

There was a pause. Nathalie spoke softly into the telephone.

"I don't want to ask what you mean by that."

Krazicek was silent for a few seconds.

"Oh, and I just wondered, does George have an address book? Like a real one, a physical one?"

"Yes, he's got this old leather thing, must go back to the eighties. Ancient. Why?"

"Let me explain when I see you; just take it."

"Krazicek, I couldn't do that. I think he would be more devastated losing that than finding out that I had been unfaithful." Nathalie felt slightly shocked.

"I understand," said Krazicek hurriedly. "Just photocopy it."

"OK." Strange, she still felt uneasy.

"One last thing Nathalie."

"Oui mon amour."

"George will know. He will know about you and me."

Nathalie's eyes widened and she suddenly felt apprehensive.

"How. He can't."

"I'm going to tell him."

He put the telephone down and looked around again. He found the plastic basin he had used earlier, filled it with cold water again and poured it over Gerhardt Teuber who awoke immediately from his exhausted slumber. Krazicek untied the cable and heaved him upright.

"OK, you've got two minutes to clean up, get yourself some disinfectant, whatever. Then I'm going to leave you with Lucas and George and you can get to know each other better...."

"They'll kill me. Don't do that, anything but that. Lock me up in another room, not with them......." Gerhardt Teuber looked and sounded frantic but shut up immediately when Krazicek roared back at him.

"You interrupt me again and I'll cut your little faggot's bollocks off. Do as I say."

Gerhardt Teuber staggered to the bathroom, found a bottle of antiseptic and, having removed his trousers poured the liquid over his wounds. Then he groaned loudly.

"Shut the fuck up you piece of Kraut shit." Krazicek rubbed his ears. "Now put some trousers on, you make me feel sick."

Teuber urinated, fished some pyjamas out of the cupboard and put them on, together with a bathrobe. He splashed his face and limped gingerly out, cringing under the towering figure of Krazicek. He proceeded meekly along the corridor to the storeroom.

Krazicek drew back the bolt and pushed Teuber ahead. Lucas and George were dozing uncomfortably on the floor. They looked up, Lucas freezing at the sight of Krazicek, forcing himself to believe what his brother had told him. Teuber stood still. A pathetic figure, humiliated and drained.

"You've stolen everything I've worked for all my life," he said to Krazicek, sounding weak and resigned.

"Yeah, well I suffer from kleptomania Gerhardt. When it gets bad I take something for it." Krazicek released a brief humourless laugh which ceased as suddenly as it had started.

"I've been wondering whether to kill you all," he continued, fondling his revolver. "If I don't then my advice to you is to not make me regret my decision. Mr Teuber, if I hear so much as a whisper from you I'll feed you to the dogs. Your fat cousin will get the same treatment and I'm not talking figuratively. Real dogs Mr Teuber."

Krazicek allowed the words to sink into Teuber's befuddled brain.

"Mr Watt senior. The notorious Lucas Watt. Any attempt to find me or denounce me or get someone to tail me and I rape your wife and strangle your children in front of her. Clear?"

Lucas stared, stunned and petrified. He just managed to nod his head.

"Mr Watt junior. George. I feel as if I know you well. Do you find that strange?"

George frowned. What a bizarre fucking question. What was he talking about? What was that smirk all about? George swayed between curiosity and a sense of dread.

"Yes," continued Krazicek, savouring the moment. "Nathalie told me a lot about you."

"What did you say?"

"Nathalie is your girlfriend's name. We got to know each other rather well while you were gallivanting around trying to steal the Teubers' money."

"You don't know Nathalie." George felt his stomach knotting up.

"Yes I do, very well in fact." Krazicek gave George an insinuating wink. "I love that little turquoise star she has tattooed just above her arse."

George leapt at his tormentor in uncontrollable rage. Krazicek neatly sidestepped him and clubbed him on the side of his head with the revolver. George toppled to the floor. He felt a heavy foot pin him to the ground. He stared up at Krazicek with as much venom as he could muster.

"Think about it George. Me fucking your girlfriend. She obviously needed a good bang. She wasn't getting quite enough from her boyfriend. You won't be seeing her again. So just cast it out of your mind. You may think you don't have much to lose so why not try and track me down. You may be right as regards yourself. But Lucas gets punished for any transgressions committed by his younger brother. Got it?"

Krazicek chuckled. "I'll send someone to let you out in a couple of days. I hope you enjoy each other's company. *Adieu.*"

The door slammed and the three men remained silent, staring at the floor of their prison.

HEADING BACK

///

KRAZICEK LOOKED ROUND the ground floor of Gerhardt Teuber's villa for a last time to check he had left nothing behind. It was just a habit, he knew there was nothing. The only object he'd brought with him was his knife and the revolver he'd picked up in San Jose. He'd already emptied Gerhardt's revolver but had thrown it into the bushes all the same, together with his own. He opened the front door, walked out to the beach and started a refreshing jog back in the direction of Tamarindo.

Despite the sand underfoot he kept up a ten kilometers per hour rhythm which brought him to the entrance of "El Bucanero" within twenty minutes. He glowed with his feeling of success, of triumph. Mind you, it hadn't been that difficult, what with Gerhardt Teuber's wimpish performance and Lucas' seizure. Now that really had been gratifying. Not to mention George's state of cuckolded indignation and bewilderment.

It was 16.00h and he entered the hotel. A somewhat ancient pitbull, obviously a permanent member of the hotel staff, wagged its tail with anomalous friendliness. A young man at the reception looked up, respect and submission instantly conveyed in his stance and smile as the handsome giant, sweating only slightly from his jog in the heat of the afternoon, approached.

"*En que puedo ayudarle Senor?*"*

"I have a message from Mr Teuber."

"Ah, Mr Teuber. Of course. We know him."

"He said there was twenty dollars for you now," Krazicek said as he pulled some notes out of his pocket, "and twenty dollars for expenses. All you have to do is go to his villa in two days time, he won't be there but the door will be unlocked, and then pick up a crate he's left in the storeroom."

"The storeroom *Senor?*"

---

* *How can I help you Sir?"*

"First on the left in the corridor as you enter the villa."

"*Si Senor.*"

"The crate has got very expensive wine in it and has an address on it in San Jose; I think it's a present for someone. You arrange for it to be sent and keep any change. All clear?"

"*Si Senor,*" confirmed the receptionist, trying not to lick his lips as he eyed the two notes on the counter.

"Now call me a taxi please."

When Krazicek got back to the Hyatt he went up to his room having ordered the taxi to wait and asked the receptionist to check on flights from Tamarindo to San Jose. If departure times were too late he would go all the way by taxi. Once there he would go straight to the airport and get the first flight to Europe.

He would take a first class seat of course, and order a bottle of champagne even if he preferred vodka. For a second he thought about Vuk and his insatiable appetite for Dom Perrignon.

He would contact his bank when he arrived.

And then he thought about Amra. He would have to kill the bitch. He owed Vuk that. He didn't relish it but it was a matter of honour. Family honour. And somehow the nearer he got to finding her the more bitter and angry he felt. That was going to help when he delivered the blow.

SWISS TRICKS

///

KRAZICEK'S BANK, United National Swiss Bank (UNSB) was not small, private and ancient like Banque Helvas, which had always thrived on old money and had an aura of tradition and even an old fashioned smell of leather and polished wood.

UNSB was a vast and sprawling international conglomerate with ambitions to become number one. This ambition led its aggressive and well-rewarded employees to cut a certain number of corners when it came to vetting potential clients.

Jacques Peletier had opened Krazicek's offshore company account back in 1994 and had managed to turn a blind eye both to the dubious nature of the company's beneficial owner and the exotic sources of funds. Large payments were credited to the account from Liberian companies, Panamanian lawyers, Vaduz Trusts and even directly from Belgrade.

No economic justification was ever given other than vague allusions to an international solar energy business. Peletier duly noted the client file and internal audit never bothered him. Indeed, as the years went by and the account grew from millions to tens of millions he was rewarded with handsome bonuses and promotion. And Krazicek would take him to lunch once a year and give him an extra sweet dessert.

While Krazicek was half way across the Atlantic, sipping champagne in accordance with his celebratory plans, the UNSB Head Office Board called Peletier to their offices in Zurich.

He was excited and looking forward to further praise and encouragement. When he got there he found the atmosphere strange however and could not understand the way he was left on his own for an hour. At last he was called to see the President of the Group no less, together with the latter's senior Board members.

"Take a seat Mr Peletier," said the President.

He began to feel nervous.

"Tell us what you know about Fairtrade Corporation Mr Peletier."

"Fairtrade?" asked Peletier stupidly.

There was a silence.

"It's a very important client Sir, it has a portfolio of over $140 million. It's the branch's most profitable relationship and has grown continuously over the last eight years." Peletier felt a drop of sweat rolling down the side of his face.

"Particularly over the last few days?"

"There were one or two significant transfers into the account this week, yes."

"How significant?"

Pelletier was now feeling very worried. He fumbled for words.

"Sixty million dollars?" Enquired the President acidly.

Pelletier nodded his head.

"And where does this extraordinary amount of money come from? We assume you have done full due diligence and maintain a log of origin of funds for all the inwards transfers?" The President stood up and started pacing round the room, stopping just behind Jacques.

"Er, yes, well, you know, when you have a long term relationship you can be a bit more flexible, take things on trust, up to a point of course."

"And what point is that Mr Peletier?"

Silence.

"I will tell you to what point," said the President with controlled fury in his voice. "To the point where your irresponsibility and total lack of respect for bank rules has led to an official enquiry from the Central bank, from TRACFIN and from the CIA. The ramifications are enormous and the potential damage to the bank's reputation incalculable. You will be questioned by the authorities this morning and held under house arrest."

Jacques Peletier felt his heart beating so hard that he couldn't find the breath to formulate a reply. His mouth was too dry anyway. He felt the hard relentless stare of the Board members' eyes. He knew exactly what the real issue was. The real issue was that the bank needed a scapegoat.

"But, but......." He at last managed to croak. "Everybody has always known about this account. The bank has never raised any objection to keeping it open....."

The President interrupted him: "If you care to go through the records you will see the file is littered with requests for you to obtain more information on the beneficial owner and verify source of funds. There are several emails from you assuring us that the file is in order and that you had personally checked on the respectability of all aspects of the relationship."

Peletier slumped back in his chair. Oh my God, they had injected stuff into his email archives. The bastards. They were going to crucify him. He was heading to prison, that was for sure, the bank would express its deep regret to the authorities about the existence of a rogue relationship manager and Krazicek was going to go ape shit.

Peletier was too panicked, for the moment, to order his thoughts around some other delicate account relationships which he knew about. Relationships which, when taken together, would make Fairtrade Corporation look like a passing distraction.

Later, when he was sitting miserably on the side of his bed with two guards outside his bedroom, he started to reflect. Fairtrade Corporation was a big account. But there were plenty more accounts in the bank which were of a similar size. And which were stuffed with funds of dubious origin. More than dubious. If he kept a cool head he might turn this knowledge to his advantage.

UNHAPPY TRIO

///

THE THREE MEN STARED AT THE FLOOR. George was the first to look up. His face was pale. Whatever his misgivings about Nathalie and however reprehensible his own behaviour in Costa Rica, the fact was he'd been cuckolded. By Vuk's brother for Christ's sake. He tried to chase away the image in his mind of Nathalie making love with Krazicek. He failed.

"He's completely humiliated all of us. Me the most."

There was silence for a moment.

"He has. But we're alive," replied Lucas. "Teuber, is there any way we can get out of here?"

Gerhardt Teuber shook his head, too shocked and depressed to speak. He started sobbing.

Lucas felt a twinge of sympathy for the man. "Let's hope Krazicek-what a ghastly name- meant it when he said he'd get someone to let us out in a couple of days." He stood up and stared at the light bulb. "And let's hope the fucking light doesn't go out. George, I think our friend needs a bit of medicine."

George nodded. "Come on Gerhardt, be a good boy, swallow some of this, it will do you good." He handed the bottle of brandy to him.

Teuber took a series of large gulps and wiped his nose with the back of his hand. The drink appeared to work its magic and his sobbing ceased. Thank God, they weren't going to murder him.

"You know what?" Said Lucas. "This feels like the Titanic. We just hit a fucking great iceberg in the shape of Krazicek and all we can do is drink brandy until the ship sinks. I've never felt so gutted."

George opened another bottle of Duque de Alba, squeamish about sharing the existing one with Gerhardt Teuber whose snot-covered face did not encourage physical intimacy of any kind.

"What about when you were driving along the Grande Corniche with Vuk in the back of the car trying to rape Chloe?"

"Yeah, that was nearly a total wipe out but I was able to do something wasn't I? I jumped the bastard and knocked him over. That allowed Chloe to grab his gun and Amra to sneak up behind. We could take some action, do something. This was different. I had some kind of seizure for God's sake, our friend Gerhardt has been cut to pieces and you've had your girlfriend....er, well, tampered with. Oh, and just in case anyone has forgotten, he nicked a cool sixty million off us. More like a fucking tsunami than an iceberg come to think of it."

Lucas sat back with the new bottle of brandy which George had passed him.

"You're doing well with the metaphors Lucas," observed George, more tired than ironic. "But what do we do now? Just sit back and wait?"

There was another silence. Gerhardt Teuber stirred.

"I've just thought of something," he said. "Belinda."

He fell silent again.

"Any chance of being a bit more explicit?" Asked Lucas.

"She's my maid."

"Pray expound Gerhardt."

"I sent her away for a few days because I knew you would be coming to.........see me. The postman told me. I didn't want her witnessing our ...."

"Confrontation?" Suggested Lucas helpfully.

"Exactly. Anyway, she will be back tomorrow. She is a conscientious worker. She checks on the storeroom every day."

"Well that's a relief. Belinda did you say?" George had perked up.

"George finds your maid very attractive, particularly her behind, not to put too fine a point on it," said Lucas.

Gerhardt Teuber looked puzzled. His Germanic mindset could not understand how, in such dire straits, anyone could be remotely interested in his maid's sexual attributes. He could have the bitch as far as he was concerned. The important thing now was to negotiate some kind of peace agreement between themselves so that they could all pick up whatever was left from Krazicek's apocalyptic passage through their lives.

Gerhardt had already gone through his accounts in his mind. He had a few million left, just like Hans. He could continue to live in Costa Rica.

BAD LOSS

///

KRAZICEK WAS BACK in the Hotel de Paris in Monaco feeling on top of the world. Everything was sorted. He would join Nathalie in Paris in two days, he'd done a magnificent job in Costa Rica, he was richer than Croesus and, the cherry on the cake......his air hostess was transiting through Nice in a few hours. A session with one of the greatest performers of crazy sex he had ever met was shortly to take place.

He sighed with self-congratulatory satisfaction, stretched his legs, took a flying somersault onto his bed and felt his body burning with invincible energy.

Maybe time to call Peletier.

Peletier's mobile telephone didn't pick up so he left a message. Jacques Peletier, in their eight year relationship, had never failed to call back within twenty minutes.

But this time he didn't call back, even after two hours. Krazicek was surprised but not worried. At 14.30h he called directly on his office number.

Peletier's telephone rang twice and a voice he did not recognize answered.

"Valérie Faure à l'appareil!"

"Pass me over to Jacques Peletier please."

"Mr Peletier has left the bank, I have taken over his accounts, how can I help you?"

"Jacques would not leave the bank without telling me."

There was a moment's silence.

"May I ask who is calling?"

"I don't know you," replied Krazicek, his voice hardening. "I only speak to Jacques. Where is he? How do I contact him? Why doesn't he pick up on his mobile?"

This was the ninth call Valérie had received since Peletier's eviction and imprisonment. She was not unaccustomed therefore to the direction the conversation was taking.

"We will be able to talk to you about Mr Peletier when you have identified yourself sir. I understand you may wish to remain anonymous over the telephone but I have all of the client secret identification codes used by Mr Peletier. You may use yours sir and then we can discuss the situation and indeed any banking business you may wish to transact."

Krazicek reflected for a moment.

"I'll call you back."

Shit, he'd called both Peletier's mobile and office numbers from his mobile. If there was trouble brewing he could be traced. And there had to be trouble brewing. That Valerie bitch would be part of any trap. He decided to call her back immediately.

"Yes, me again. Look, I think it's better if I come into your office and you explain exactly what's going on. I'll be there tomorrow morning, I'll be driving from Monaco, leaving in about ten minutes. In the meantime I want an urgent $10 million transfer made to another company account in Panama. Here's the code."

Valérie Faure was a bright girl but she hesitated long enough to confirm Krazicek's bad feeling.

"Yes of course. Perhaps you will be good enough to sign the instruction tomorrow. It's a large amount you understand so I will have to wait for your signature."

Krazicek held the mobile away as he spat on the floor with rage. His arrangements were clear, there were no limits on telephonic instructions as long as the code was right.

"I understand everything," he said quietly. "I will see you tomorrow at 10.00h sharp if that is convenient?"

Valérie could barely disguise her breathlessness. This was going to be a major hit. Police, journalists, CIA, the anti-fraud squad. She was going to be famous.

****

Krazicek put his mobile phone in an envelope, leaving it switched on. He went downstairs, through the lobby and walked to the nearest taxi.

"I have an unusual request for you. Are you free to drive to Geneva now?"

"Yes Sir," replied the delighted driver.

"Take this envelope, don't worry it's only an expensive mobile phone, and drop it off at the address I've written down here. Here's one thousand Euros. Don't let me down, it belongs to my wife."

"Comme si c'était fait Monsieur. Merci."

Krazicek walked quickly back into the hotel and settled his bill. He retrieved his luggage which had barely been unpacked and walked back to the front of the Hotel de Paris. He had been going to get the train but another taxi was already waiting in front of the hotel and he told the driver to take him to Nice.

"When I said Nice, I meant the airport," he said to the driver.

"J'allais vous demander Monsieur. Pas de probléme. Vous partez loins?" *

"Baghdad," Krazicek replied without thinking.

The taxi driver looked at him wryly in the rear view mirror.

"Baghdad is very much in fashion at the moment," he said.

The taxi glided smoothly through the exit tunnel connecting Monaco to France, climbed the dual carriageway to the next tunnel and exited through the tollgate to the motorway. Krazicek swore under his breath. The full extent of the disaster was sinking in.

"How free are you for a long trip?" He asked.

"Now *Monsieur*?"

"Yeah, now. I'm fed up with airplanes. I have to go via Paris to get a decent connection to Baghdad. Can you drive me there?"

"Avec plaisir Monsieur." ***

---

* *"Consider it done Sir. Thank you."*

** *"I was going to ask Sir. No problem. Are you travelling far?"*

*** *"With pleasure Sir"*

Krazicek sat back. He had to think calmly. He made a few calculations. There was his account in Spain, one and a half million Euros there, plus his account in Panama. His arms dealer contacts remained in place. He'd never be short of cash. But he was no longer in the financial stratosphere if, as he guessed, his account had been discovered by the authorities.

He thought about the airhostess for a moment. He shrugged resignedly and pulled out his replacement mobile. Another thing he'd learnt from Vuk.

At least there was a warm pair of arms waiting for him in Paris. And Nathalie would have the photocopied pages of George's diary. So he would be able to find Amra.

The vicious little Bosnian bitch remained at the top of his list of priorities despite his personal financial meltdown. He had deliberately avoided asking Lucas or George how to find her. He might have forced an answer out of them but they would have warned her. Unless he'd shot them both. But that wasn't quite his style.

But if shooting people wasn't quite his style was he going to be able to make an exception with Amra? Of course he was. He gritted his teeth and let the hate swell up again.

RELEASE

WHILE KRAZICEK WAS BEING DRIVEN to Paris the sun was coming up over Costa Rica. Playa Grande sparkled, a light breeze swept across the Pacific, just enough to sway the palm trees, and a beautiful young woman walked barefoot along the shore.

Belinda had enjoyed her stay in San Jose. She'd seen family and friends, bought presents for everyone, danced until early in the morning and helped her mother clean and paint her little flat which she rented in the Barrio Otoya. The neighbourhood was full of historic buildings, boutique hotels and restaurants but the flat was in a ramshackle building down a side street and cost only USD 120 a month.

She sniffed the air, an exhilarating contrast to the exhaust fumes of San Jose. Then she frowned slightly. The idea of seeing Gerhardt Teuber again and being subjected to his scary sexual routine was not a pleasant one. She stopped and looked out to sea. Maybe she should turn round now, find another job somewhere else. But where?

She undressed, ran into the water and felt cleansed as she dived into the churning white foam. She swam strongly towards the big waves, pummelled and shaken like a doll every time the surf hit her. After twenty minutes she allowed herself to be swept back towards the shore. She looked for her clothes and then realised the current had taken her a full two hundred metres further up the beach. She jogged back, enjoying the feel of her young breasts moving with her stride. She was dry within a few minutes and reluctantly put her clothes back on.

Gerhardt Teuber's villa had its downstairs lights on. Belinda looked at her watch and frowned. *Mierda, ya se ha levantado.*[*] She walked to her little hut at the bottom of the garden and entered. She didn't have a key, there was no lock and apart from a tiny radio

---

[*]   *"Shit, he's already got out of bed."*

and some simple kitchen utensils there was virtually nothing of the slightest value. Apart from her pictures.

She used most of her spare time for drawing and painting. Everything she saw in the forest, both fauna and fauna, she reproduced on paper with her own technique and innocent style.

The most exciting colours, the ones she loved most, and the greatest source of pleasure, she had found with the frogs. There were supposed to be nearly two hundred species of frog and she had already come across thirty of them. The Blue Jeans frog, the Red Eyed Leaf frog, the Milk frog....she had rendered them with attention to the slightest detail and always against a dreamy background of trees and flowers, a sort of Garden of Eden which had formed itself in her mind from those early years when she had sat, wide eyed, listening to bible lessons.

She smiled when she saw the pictures stacked against the wall. She decided she would move on to something fresh. She had already drawn some birds, mainly toucans and macaws. But she had never drawn pelicans, despite the fact she spent so much time watching them. This would be her next theme.

Belinda looked at her tiny plastic watch. It was already 07.00h. Time to let the master know she was back. She ran a comb through her damp hair and then swept it back in a ponytail with her hands, tying it firmly with a blue ribbon. She always imagined this practical style might help her escape Gerhardt Teuber's libidinous eye. She was unaware that it only enhanced her beauty and emphasised her youth.

She walked reluctantly up the path, past the banana trees, towards the front of the villa. There was something incongruous about the lights and the total silence. Surely the man was up and about? She came tentatively round the side of the house and recoiled as she saw the smashed window of the study. Her heart began to beat fast and she covered her mouth with her hand.

Very frightened now, she nevertheless found the courage to crane her head forward and look inside. The shambles which Krazicek had left behind was complete, nothing seemed to have been spared. And the blood everywhere made her feel sick. Very sick. She retched and felt the acid in her throat.

She stayed immobile for a few minutes and gathered her shattered wits. Whatever had happened had clearly taken place at least a couple of days ago. The blood was dry.

She waited to see if the silence continued. She strained her ears but could hear nothing. After ten minutes she tiptoed past the broken window and entered the villa through the front door which was wide open. She poked her head into the study but saw nothing she had not already noticed from when she was outside.

She looked down the corridor towards the bathroom and kitchen and walked gingerly towards them. As she went past the storeroom she thought she heard some voices. Male voices. She felt her pulse pick up again immediately and froze.

Weird, the door was closed and bolted so how come there were people inside? She pressed her ear against the door and thought she could just make out Gerhardt Teuber's voice. She continued listening for a moment. Yes, it was him. And there were at least two other voices.

What should she do? Call the police? She thought about it. If Teuber was there he was obviously a prisoner. Maybe he'd been locked up by the burglars. Worse than burglars judging from the mess in the study. And whoever was locked up with him were by definition prisoners too. So nobody was going to hurt her if she opened the door.

She slid back the bolt, ready to run, and pulled the door open. The three men stopped talking and stared, eyes wide. Gerhardt Teuber was sitting down with his legs covered in dry blood and bruises on his face, torn clothes and grey stubble. A large man stood behind him. He looked in reasonable shape but had dark rings under his eyes and also a couple of days of greyish beard.

A younger man stood next to him, dark stubble this time, and was looking at her strangely. Then she recognized the look. The man obviously found her attractive, very attractive. That was bizarre, not because she wasn't used to admiring looks from men but because it was as if he already knew her.

But she didn't have time to analyse things. The situation itself was totally bizarre and she was bursting with anxious curiosity.

"What has happened *Senor*?"

Gerhardt Teuber closed his eyes, opened them again, blinked and wondered what to say.

"We got hit by a tsunami Senorita," said Lucas. "And you have saved us. Thank you."

Belinda looked and sounded puzzled. "A tsunami Senor?"

"Just a figure of speech," said George with what she thought was a very warm smile. What the hell did 'figure of speech' mean anyway?

"Call a doctor Belinda. *En seguida por favour.*" Now that the nightmare appeared to be drawing to a close Gerhardt Teuber seemed to be wilting into a state of post-traumatic shock.

"*Si Senor.*" Belinda rushed to the telephone.

Lucas and George rushed to the bathroom.

---

*   *"Immediately please."*

FIND AMRA

NATHALIE SAT ON THE KING SIZED BED of the best suite in the Hotel George V and felt her whole body burning with excitement. Krazicek had telephoned to say he was already on the outskirts of Paris approaching the Porte d'Orleans from the south. He would be with her in about half an hour.

She stood up and looked at herself in the mirror for the third time. She had never looked so good. Her infatuation with Krazicek seemed to have drawn out a profoundly hidden beauty which softened her features and added expression to her eyes and mouth. She cupped her breasts in her hands and pouted at herself. Then she lifted her skirt and ran her hands over her thighs.

There was only one small cloud which occasionally skimmed across her consciousness and troubled her otherwise total serenity: the address book. The photocopy lay in her suitcase. Why did Krazicek want it? She felt guilty. More guilty than she felt about her infidelity to George. But that wasn't difficult.

When the knock on the door occurred her heartbeat accelerated and her doubts receded. She opened it and looked at the man who had made her into a woman and threw herself into his arms. His hands quickly descended from her back down to her buttocks.

She let herself be taken and revelled in his desire. She forgot everything and thought about love. When she came she always cried "Yes" except this time she cried louder.

"Baby," said Krazicek. "You are the most amazing woman I've ever met. I just want to fuck you and fuck you and fuck you."

"I know," she replied demurely.

"That's all part of the language of love," he said. "Even vulgar words are love words."

Nathalie looked at him, fascinated.

"You understand?"

"Yes."

"Drink?"

"Mmm."

In what seemed a now familiar routine Krazicek got out of bed and made his way to the mini bar. Both sensed a tiny subliminal tension which needed to be dispelled. Krazicek's enormous hand withdrew a bottle of Dom Perignon and Nathalie watched, entranced, as he peeled off the foil and allowed the cork to push itself out, smothered and controlled, all in a single movement.

"Oh God!"

"What's the matter?" Asked Krazicek.

"Just the way you open the champagne. It turns me on."

He laughed. "Never thought of it that way."

They settled together on the bed and looked at each other. Nathalie started with a sip which turned into a gulp. Krazicek swallowed his glass in a second and poured himself some more. He felt the tension easing out of his body.

"Lot of things happened since I saw you. Just a few days but crazy days."

"Krazicek days," she said softly.

"You got it."

They looked at each other and drank some more champagne. Nathalie suddenly laughed.

"If you're waiting for me to ask you what the hell you've been doing....."

Krazicek laughed too. "There's been a lot of money circulating around, it went into Lucas and George's account and then it left to go into my account. And then I lost everything, including my previous savings."

He told her the story.

Nathalie sat back on the bed feeling numb, staring at him with unblinking eyes. "You lost a hundred and forty five million dollars?"

Krazicek nodded.

"And all you can think about is fucking me and drinking champagne?"

Krazicek nodded.

"I love you."

"Don't get romantic, I just love your arse."

Nathalie shrieked with laughter and jumped on him, upsetting the Dom Perrignon. He picked up the foaming bottle, drank out of it and then let the clear bubbling liquid out of his mouth as his tongue searched frantically between her thighs. They made love again and then she fell asleep.

Five minutes later Nathalie's lover quietly got out of bed and started a methodical search of the hotel suite for the information he wanted.

He took only a few minutes to find the photocopied pages of George's battered little address book in Nathalie's suitcase. And he took a few seconds more to find the page with the name he was looking for.

There were several mobile numbers which had been scratched out and only one which was left intact. All the addresses had been crossed out but were still legible.

He sat down at the desk and folded the page and placed it carefully inside his jacket which was hanging on the back of the chair. Then he poured himself a strong vodka and tonic and started planning his trip.

As usual he noted down key points:

1/ Travel

2/ Locate A.

3/ The kill.

He considered each question, sipping his drink. He preferred total independence and considered driving all the way. Too far. He pulled up a map of Europe on the computer screen and decided to fly to Venice and hire a car there. The drive to Bosnia would take a few hours and he would travel on his other Dutch passport. Nobody spoke Dutch except the Dutch so it was the best cover. Jon Vanhouteghem suddenly no longer existed. *Yerfdog De Vries* suddenly came to life. Ridiculous names they had in the Netherlands. Too bad.

He wasn't sure about how best to contact Amra. If he did it himself she might recognize his voice. He wasn't Vuk's identical twin for nothing. He could bribe someone to call and find out her whereabouts. Someone in Bosnia, who spoke her native language. Maybe some pretext to do with delivering a parcel? Too corny? Bosnia Herzogovina was so small he was bound to find her anyway. Just ask around, sniff her out, hunt her down and then kill the bitch.

Whichever way she died he wanted her to know that this was her punishment for what she had done to Vuk. So a sniper's bullet was too simple, too easy on her. He would have to confront her himself, pour out his rage and hatred, make her understand.

There were many ways to kill her. He thought about strangling her. Would he be capable of it? He pictured her, powerless in his grip, the look of recognition in her eyes as she slowly lost consciousness and died. He pictured her falling to the ground.

He went to the bathroom, relieved himself, splashed some cold water on his face and looked in the mirror. There were no signs of fatigue on his strong handsome face but he knew he was tired. He rubbed his chin and decided to go back to bed without waking up Nathalie.

She was an amazing lay, no doubt about that, but if he woke her up she'd be all over him again and he needed sleep. He decided to spend two days in Paris before leaving for Venice. He would sleep well, eat well, take a bit of time off while his subconscious worked out the details of his Bosnian trip.

Nathalie was fast asleep. She was breathing peacefully, making a purring noise. He watched her face, sensed the smooth dry skin and felt an unfamiliar pang of tenderness.

Shit, he was falling in love with the bitch. He smiled into the darkness. There's a first time for everything in life.

TIME OFF

///

GEORGE CONSIDERED HIS POSSIBILITIES and quickly discovered he didn't want to think at all. He felt the delicious contradiction between the enormous offense of Nathalie's infidelity and his newfound liberty; he owed her nothing now and his Costa Rican frolicking no longer carried any sense of guilt.

He and Lucas decided to stay on in Tamarindo for two weeks. Both felt an urge to pamper their tired bodies and minds. And they were worried about returning too quickly to France. Those transfers of tens of millions of dollars had to have left a trace. It was not the initial receipt of thirty million dollars from Hans Teuber. It was the almost immediate transfer out of the same amount to Fairtrade Corporation. Somewhere, some monitoring agency might have spotted it.

Chloe was given the number of their hotel and asked to call from a phone booth. Lucas felt the soothing balm of her love and calm and after he had put the phone down promised himself he would never deceive her again. George raised an eyebrow but concluded he was sincere.

"Are you judging me?" Lucas asked

"Not at all, I'm proud of you in a way. You're a randy bastard but seem to be able to reconcile that with being a loving husband and father."

"I like that George. Thank you. Maybe I should continue in the same manner."

"And maybe not."

Three days slipped by in a timeless way. Both men got fit again, Lucas ahead, ruthlessly cutting out any alcohol. Only the weight of his years prevented him from finishing in front when they jogged ten kilometres a day through the heavy sand and swam through the surf for over two hours a day.

George's only source of frustration was Belinda's surprising resistance to his gentlemanly approaches. There was something in the way, a barrier that he couldn't understand. She was totally free because Gerhardt had travelled to Liechtenstein to lick his wounds and discuss the way forward with his cousin Hans. So what was holding her back?

They spent many hours together on the beach, Belinda teaching him how to surf. He was surprisingly clumsy and never managed to get beyond standing on his board until after the waves had broken, using the foaming white water to propulse him towards the shore. The physical intimacy of swimming and surfing together and sometimes even clinging together if they were swept over by a particularly powerful wave did not serve as a premise to having sex together and George's ardour remained unrequited.

When he had tried for the second time to kiss her and she turned her head gently, inoffensively, to one side, he sighed and looked at her sweet profile, perplexed.

"Que te pasa Belinda, porque no me dejas besarte?"

*"Porque si te dejo, luego me vas a hacer el amor. Yo me voy a enamorar de ti y tu vas a regresar en tu pais, dejandome sola y triste. Gracias pero no!"***

So that was it! He felt a mixture of relief and hesitation. This was the moment when he could try and talk her into it. But if he denied going back to France one day that would be a lie (an obvious one). If he asked her to go back with him that was tantamount to proposing marriage. Better pursue the charm offensive.

"Belinda, you are young and beautiful, I'm not so young and not so beautiful....we're very complementary when you think about it."

She laughed.

"I think we could have fun without anyone getting hurt."

---

*   *What's wrong belinda, why won't you let me kiss you?"*

**   *"Because if I let you kiss me you will make love to me. I will fall in love and then you will go back to your country, leaving me lonely and sad. Thanks, but no."*

She nodded wisely at him. "Without *you* getting hurt."

Lucas in the meantime started to express a degree of boredom with the repetitive nature of their daily routine; at the end of the fourth day sitting at the hotel bar sipping a diet Coke, he asked George to join him the following morning for a trip further south.

"How much further south?"

"We're going to explore Nicoya, the whole peninsula, keeping mainly to the coast. There's a place called Malpais where the beaches are amazing and the food is all locally grown and organic. We'll call Chloe and Jérôme when we get there to give our new hotel telephone number."

"OK. I get it." George thought wistfully about Belinda for a minute and decided the time had indeed come for a move.

TARGET

THE MOUNTAINS OVERLOOKING SARAJEVO, from where the city was shelled to cinders and snipers had picked off harmless citizens, were beautiful. But you could picnic there now, take a stroll, sniff the clean air.

It was unbearably sad, thought Amra, that several years on, Bosnia-Herzegovina still had nothing but the labels "war-torn" and "troubled". For Bosnia-Herzegovina war did not seem able to become part of its history, no phoenix had arisen from the ashes and somehow the memory of suffering seemed to have generated such political and economic dysfunction that the country was mired in a blighted malaise.

There was little opportunity for those interested in progress and reconciliation. Attempts at forming political parties that strove for the rule of law and multi-ethnic co-existence had proved fruitless. Bosnia was more divided now than before the civil war.

Amra sat back and sighed as she felt the last dregs of hope and enthusiasm drain out of her. She looked around her hotel room and decided she had had enough. She had thought she loved Sarajevo. She had. But her relationship with the city now, after so many years, was like that of an overwrought couple whose frustrations had slowly sucked away energy and hope. She no longer believed in the future. She needed to get away. She needed to see George.

Her mobile rang. A polite voice. Vaguely familiar.

"Is this Amra ?"

"What can I do for you ?"

"I work for 'Save Bosnia', a UK charity funded by the government. We're recognized by the UN. They gave us a list of contacts, one of whom was you. They said we had to start by talking to you, that you knew more about the country than most. We have significant funds and we need to make sure they are used properly."

Amra paused. Another charity. She felt a flicker of interest despite her despondency.

"Well, I'll be pleased to help with basic guidance but we'll have to meet in the next few days, I'm leaving the country soon. May not be back for a while."

The pleasant voice expressed relief that they had been lucky enough to find her before she left. They could arrange a meeting whenever it suited her.

Amra agreed and said Sarajevo would be the most convenient place for her.

"That's perfect," replied the nice voice. "We have a room at the Astra hotel which we use as a base. We've converted it into a sort of office. Not very grand, a couple of desks and a computer, coffee machine, you know."

"That's fine by me. Can you make tomorrow?"

"Sure. 11.30h at the hotel? Thank you Amra. When you get there just ask for Yerfdog De Vries. The room's booked in my name."

Amra put her mobile down and shrugged her shoulders. It would be nice in a way. One last gesture to help her poor divided country before she left for France.

Definitely the last, she'd done her best and now she had to live her own life. She switched off her mobile with a feeling of deep fatigue. No more calls.

SUDDEN DOUBTS

KRAZICEK'S DEPARTURE FROM PARIS left Nathalie with a feeling of emptiness, tinged with anxiety. She was in love with a man she barely knew, a self-avowed arms trafficker, the twin brother of a mass murderer. This was a disturbing way of summarizing things.

Much as she tried, she couldn't quite put the positive spin on the strange man that she needed to reassure herself. Nor could she rid herself of a feeling of hiatus, of being stranded with no tangible plan or destination. But she missed him, she needed him. His strength. No man could quite match up to Krazicek. Her heart softened.

He had said she could stay on at the George V but she found the luxury of the room and the uniquely French haughtiness of the staff oppressing. The Champs Elysées where the hotel was situated made her feel depressed, the plethora of chic boutiques juxtaposed with cinemas and burger joints and the endless swirl of traffic and tourists giving her a sensation of claustrophobia.

Krazicek had pressed several thousand Euros into her hand before leaving to sort out some "unfinished business". She went up to her room after breakfast (he had left very early) and decided to move to somewhere more simple and cheerful. The left bank. That would do. She knew the whole *Quartier Latin* well. She had lived near the Bd. St. Michel as a student, in fact right up to when she had met George nearly eight years ago.

She looked at the rumpled bed and felt an immediate twinge of excitement. Their two days together had been like living on another planet, completely divorced from any reality other than their physical passion, expensive champagne and exquisite cuisine.

They had made love on the first morning, crossed the Champs Elysées to lunch at Fouquets, crossed back to return to bed, sleep and then emerge late in the evening to dine at the Tour d'Argent.

The second day was not dissimilar so Krazicek's departure that morning left a vacuum.

She picked up her suitcase and placed it on the bed, having stripped away the sheets and eiderdown. Then she started neatly preparing her clothes. One little pile for underwear, another for two dresses and a pair of jeans. She brushed her teeth and assembled her modest collection of toiletries and makeup. Then she made a separate pile for her passport, a novel she was reading and various documents. She always put such items in the zipped pocket of her suitcase when she travelled.

She picked up the photocopied pages of George's address book, which were still at the bottom of the case where she had left them when she had unpacked. She sat down on the bed, holding them in her hand. A nagging nostalgia. Nearly eight years with George. She didn't regret leaving him but time had left an indelible impression of him somewhere in her mind and heart. Dear George, she really didn't want him to suffer. How on earth had he felt when Krazicek had told him about her infidelity?

She thumbed the pages, briefly registering the names of friends they had in common. She found her own name, obviously added to the address book after their first meeting on the train from London to Paris. All that time ago. She saw Lucas' secretary's name, Solange. She had always been a bit jealous of her. She saw Jérôme's, Lucas' and Chloe's mobile numbers.

She thumbed through to what should have been the first page. It was missing. She shrugged and then she frowned. The first page, A for Amra. She went through all the pages again. It was not to be found. She tried to force away the thoughts cascading through her head. She failed.

Oh God, she had told Krazicek everything. She had told him who had killed his brother. His twin brother. He'd left that morning with Amra's mobile number. He was going to track her down and wreak revenge. Kill her maybe. Certainly. And it would be her fault. Amra was going to die because of her. She put her face in her hands and felt an icy thrust of terror and remorse. Everything she had done in the last few weeks seemed despicable.

As her panic subsided, only to be replaced by a numbing sense of dread and horror, her brain cleared slightly and she could find only one course of action. She had to warn Amra. And the only person she could contact who would have her mobile number and be able to call her was George. But George and Lucas were not picking up on their mobiles in Costa Rica because of some complication which neither she nor Chloe fully understood. But Chloe had their hotel number.

She picked up her mobile with trembling hands and called her.

"Chloe, c'est moi."

"Nathalie? I thought you'd left for good. I didn't expect to hear from you again." Chloe's voice was cold.

Nathalie started sobbing. An invisible wall now separated her from her previous life. From normality, sanity, safety. She controlled her tears and spoke.

"Chloe, there have been some crazy things going on in my life." She paused. That *crazy* word again. "You've got to 'phone Lucas and George, I can't do it, not after what has happened. Terrible things."

"What has happened that is so terrible?" Chloe sounded alarmed.

"Never mind how, but I met Vuk's twin Brother."

Chloe seemed to choke. "No, no, please tell me that is not true."

"Don't worry, everybody is safe, he doesn't want to kill you or Lucas or me or George. But he wants to find Amra. He found out it was she who pulled the trigger....."

"He can't have. Only we know about that."

"I told him. I told him the whole story because I had no idea he was Vuk's twin. Then he stole George's address book. He's going to find Amra. He's going to kill her and it's my fault."

She could almost hear Chloe trembling on the other end of the line.

"Listen Chloe. I don't have Amra's mobile number, only George has got it. You've got to contact him. Do it now."

"I can't Nathalie. They left the hotel where I had their number. Lucas said they were going to travel South. He said he would call me to give me a new number. There's nothing I can do, they don't pick up on their mobiles."

"Oh God."

Nathalie hung up without saying goodbye.

CLOSING IN

KRAZICEK CLIMBED BACK into his rented Golf with satisfaction. He called the Astra Hotel and reserved a suite. Then he called his one contact in Sarajevo. The one contact who would do anything he asked.

Dmitri had been at school with Krazicek. An intelligent boy, nice looking but physically weak and too often the prey of bigger stronger boys who regularly bullied and humiliated him. Krazicek and Vuk decided to help him, not because they particularly liked him but because Vuk knew he could enjoy himself by inflicting pain and punishment on his tormentors and Krazicek automatically tagged along with his brother. The twins were the same age as the other boys involved but already four inches taller than average.

It had been a typical day. Dmitri had been cornered by his schoolmates close to the school exit. He was carrying his satchel, walking as quickly as possible in the direction of home. Five large boys, all about twelve years old, preadolescent and tough, followed him for about a hundred metres down the narrow street. One of them snatched his satchel and threw it on the ground. Another spat at him. The remaining three came close, chewing gum.

"Going back to see Mummy?"

The group had not looked behind them. If they had they might have acted differently. Vuk and Krazicek were following. Dmitri was thrown to the ground and the biggest of the five boys placed a large booted foot on his chest. The others started pulling his trousers off.

"Having fun?"

The boys spun round and saw the twins. A moment of hesitation. They were five, the twins were two. Dmitri didn't count.

"Fuck off, mind your own business," replied the boy holding Dmitri to the ground.

Vuk approached calmly, seized his arm, twisted it brutally until he heard it crack and summoned his brother who was grinning in the background.

"Krazicek, I think this guy has hurt his arm. Got any first aid you can apply?"

"Sure thing Vuk, don't want to see any unnecessary suffering." He walked up to the screaming boy and punched him hard in the stomach. The screaming stopped as the boy lay helplessly winded on the ground. Krazicek felt sick. He was forcing himself to please his brother. This was going further than he liked. He reminded himself of what the wounded boy had been doing to Dmitri.

The other boys remained silent, immobilised by their fear. They couldn't even run for it because Krazicek had positioned himself in front and Vuk had quickly taken up the rear. They backed away as Krazicek approached.

One was hit violently on the back of the head by Vuk's fist. Another went down with a second punch from Vuk to his face to see three of his teeth spin out in front of him onto the street. The remaining two begged for mercy. They were told to kneel down. They did.

"Who's your best friend then?" Asked Vuk.

Silence. The boys looked at each other in confusion.

Vuk pulled them both by their hair to where Dmitri was standing. He pushed their faces down to Dmitri's feet.

"Start licking and don't stop until I tell you. Then tell me who your best friend is."

When they were told to stop they knew the answer.

"Dmitri is our best friend."

And so it was that Dmitri considered he owed the twins a life long debt.

When Krazicek asked him to book and kit out a hotel room that day with desks and computers he asked no questions and did as he was bid.

"There will be a girl coming to the room asking for the 'Save Bosnia' charity. She will come at 11.30h. Tomorrow. I want you to show her in, make her feel at home, give her a coffee. Tell her Yerfdog De Vries is a few minutes late. When she's seated with the coffee you can leave. I'll be there when you come, say 10.30h. but I'll be hiding in the bedroom while you deal with the girl."

Dmitri smiled to himself. Trust Krazicek. The twins had always had phenomenal success with women. God knows what the desks and computers were all about.

Krazicek started his short journey to Sarajevo. He had 24 hours to prepare for the kill. He threw his mobile out of the car window. Nobody was going to track him now. Not when he was so near to strangling the bitch.

He felt the fury and the pain coursing through his veins.

DESPERATE

///

NATHALIE STARED AT HERSELF in the mirror as if to find an answer to her conflicting thoughts. Then she finished packing, snapped shut her case and walked quickly to the lift. Krazicek had paid in advance for the room until the following week so she walked past reception directly out onto Avenue George V. Several taxis were waiting.

"Orly s'il vous plaît."

Nice was her only possible destination. There were hourly flights from Orly airport. She could be there by midday and she still had the keys to the flat. She had left George's address book on his desk. Thank God. She would be able to call Amra herself. The thought calmed her.

She couldn't quite situate Bosnia Herzegovina on the map but knew it was part of Yugoslavia. What had been Yugoslavia before the civil war. And Yugoslavia bordered Italy. So he could already be there because she knew he had taken a 6.00 a.m. flight to Venice. She felt the panic rising again and needed a cigarette.

The taxi pulled up at the airport at 10.45h. She handed a hundred Euro bank note to the driver and ran into the Orly Sud terminal without waiting for the change. The flight departure display panel showed an 11.20h Air France flight to Nice. Rush hour was over and nobody was queuing at the Air France counter. She paid cash for a one-way ticket to Nice and just made it to the departure lounge as the check in closed behind her.

She settled in her seat, the Boeing 737 lifted off and she tried to gather her circular and repetitive thoughts again. She had to be totally mad. She knew enough about Vuk from George. A brutal murderer who had played a major role in the ethnic cleansing which the Serbs had initiated in Bosnia not even ten years ago. And she'd taken his brother as her lover. His twin brother!

As the plane started the familiar descent towards Nice she felt the tears rising to her eyes. How many times had she flown in and out of Nice, looking down on St. Tropez, the islands nearby and the coastline dotted with villas and swimming pools. They flew low over Cannes. A picture of herself and George, hand in hand, in love.

By the time she descended from her taxi in front of his apartment on Mont Boron it was exactly 13.00h. She looked around furtively, feeling like an intruder. She was. She groped in her bag and pulled out the set of keys.

Inside she was met by the strange tangible emptiness of a place deserted. Everything was in place apparently but a silent voice seemed to proclaim abandon. In just a few days the atmosphere had changed from lively to lifeless. She felt afraid. Her scribbled note to George stood propped up on the bar:

George, I'm sorry if this gives you a shock but I'm leaving Nice and leaving you. Things are no longer the same, you know that. Thanks for all the good times, that's what I will remember, I will not allow the bad times to get started. Bonne vie, Nathalie.

She walked over to the little study where they kept their correspondence and various documents. A laptop computer sat neatly in the middle of the desk and in one of the little alcoves was the address book. She picked it up and found Amra's number.

What was she going to say? It was almost with relief that she heard the answering machine. Amra's calm, measured voice requesting her to call back later or leave a message. She couldn't formulate everything she had to say. She felt strangely inhibited. Then she tried again, some ten minutes later. Again, the answering machine.

She stared helplessly at her telephone and decided to send a text. How the hell did you tell a total stranger that someone was going to murder her? Just do it. She started tapping in her message.

Please believe this is not a joke. Vuk's brother has found out it was you. He has your mobile number and he's coming for you now. You must disappear immediately. I'm Nathalie, George's girlfriend (ex). Tell me you got this text. It's my fault, I will do anything to stop him.

She smoked a cigarette and waited for a reply.

Suddenly her mobile started ringing.

"Hello?"

She heard Cloe's voice, urgent.

"Nath, Lucas called. He passed me over to George when I told him what happened. George got a bit hysterical. He's on his way now to San José, that's going to take hours, then he's getting a flight to Sarajevo via Madrid. He won't be back for nearly two days. He said Amra lives in Sarajevo but she keeps changing apartment and she's not picking up on her mobile. He's panicking......He's going to call you in a few minutes."

Nathalie remained silent for a few seconds. Then she decided.

"I'll go to Sarajevo myself. Tell George not to worry, not to call. There's nothing he can do. I'll find her."

As soon as she'd hung up she felt the surge of certainty about what she should do seep away.

She started looking for flights to Sarajevo. There weren't any except from Paris. Shit, she should have stayed there. Then she found a flight to Dubrovnik from Nice. It was leaving at 18.30h.

Then her mobile rang again. George's number flashed up. She couldn't pick up, he was going to ask how Krazicek got Amra's number. Her treachery was too great. She let the mobile ring and then waited for the inevitable message. George's voice had never sounded so dangerous.

You have to go to Sarajevo, you have to find Amra. Keep calling her, texting her. I'm on the way to San Jose but it's going to be too late by the time I get back. Amra is known to people in the United Nations envoy in Bosnia. Lucas is working on this, he has a senior contact in Geneva whose going to put out an alert and locate the people she knows.

There was a pause. Then George's voice rose higher, she could hear the latent hysteria.

You are responsible for this you stupid bitch. You've signed her death warrant, now you have to save her. If you don't I'll never forgive you. Nobody will. Go find your new boyfriend, call him, make him hold back somehow. If you don't you will be an accomplice to murder.

Another pause.

Maybe you already are.

She put her mobile down and felt the acid burning in her stomach. George had broken any semblance of the self-control which she had tried so hard to maintain. She fell to her knees and cried for nearly ten minutes, huge terrified sobs as she bit into her knuckles.

She managed to stand up, hunched and weak. She went to the bar and poured herself a cognac. The cliché flitted across her mind. She felt better almost immediately and drained the glass greedily.

Her mind cleared and she thought about calling Krazicek. But he hardly ever picked up on his mobile; he always waited for a message. And he was so smart. What could she do? Pretend to be ill and tell him he had to come back to France immediately? Reveal that she knew what he was planning and beg for mercy? She knew nothing would work.

She flipped back to the Austrian Airways web site and booked her flight. She could be in Dubrovnik by 19.30h. Another three hours at that time of day and she would have had time to drive to Sarajevo. Maybe Amra would have picked up on her messages by then. Maybe the UN would have found her. Maybe.

Maybe she was already too late. And what the hell could she do anyway?

****

Nine hours later she dropped exhausted on her hotel bed in Sarajevo. She had to sleep. She would allow herself that. Peter Dyson, Amra's friend and contact within the UN, had contacted her just before she boarded her flight from Nice. He had sounded worried but matter of fact. He was neutral with her. Maybe he didn't know she was responsible for everything. She would call him as soon as she awoke.

TOO SLOW

///

GEORGE'S JOURNEY BACK WAS BAD. Everything conspired to lend a nightmarish *lenteur* to each phase. Lucas drove him from the Santa Teresa beach in Nicoya to the ferry at Paquera, but they arrived a minute late to see the metal bridge used to board it being slowly withdrawn as the ferry left for Puntarenas, leaving them behind in a cloud of indifferent diesel fumes.

They sat in silence as the blurred outline of the next ferry came into sight several miles away.

The crossing was agonisingly slow and once they got to the other side the jumble of lorries parked in front of them, on the ferry's lower deck which was reserved for vehicles, took a clumsy twenty minutes to disembark. The relaxed Costa Rican existentialism they had grown to love began to rankle.

Lucas lit one of his rare cigarettes and gathered his thoughts as he observed the tranquil disorder.

"When you think about it George, the whole thing is going to have played itself out by the time you get there. And even if you managed to get there in time......well, in time for what? If nobody has found Amra then you're not going to either. If they have found her then she's been saved. Getting the next plane or the one after doesn't change a bloody thing. So cool down for Christ's sake."

George felt a familiar mixture of exasperation and resentment. His brother had a way applying common sense devoid of any sentiments which grated with him, even if he had to acknowledge that he frequently did the same thing. They'd inherited the habit from their military father.

"I'm just fucking worried, can't help that."

"How close a friend is she?" Asked Lucas.

"Right now she feels like the only friend I care about on the whole planet. So I guess that means very close."

"You don't think you're blowing things up in your mind? I mean since Nath left you and went off with that psychopath and

Belinda failed to surrender to your manly charm, you don't think Amra has suddenly become.... more important?" Lucas' words were slightly ironic but his tone was sincere.

"Who cares? I just love her Lucas, I don't know why we didn't stay together. She had to go to Bosnia, do her thing, help her people. Nathalie rolled up in Nice at the same time as Amra left which made it easier to forget her. And so we lost seven years when we could have been together.

"And now she might get wiped out by that bastard Krazicek who tracked her down by screwing my girlfriend, who gave him my address book. I'll kill her if anything happens. I'll strangle her with my own bare hands......"

George covered his eyes with his hands as he tried not to cry.

Lucas looked on with alarm and sorrow. "Shit man, I haven't seen you cry since you were about the age of six. And that was because I hid your teddy bear."

George gave a brief snort of laughter. He took a small swig out of the bottle of Centenario which Lucas had had the foresight to put in the back of the car when they had set off from Santa Teresa that morning. He regained his self-control and stared resignedly at the traffic.

San José airport was three hours away. The flight, if he didn't miss it was in four and a half hours. Then another ten hours to Madrid. Lucas would work out the best onward connections to Sarajevo and text him the details.

From the moment he had spoken to Chloe and his final arrival in Sarajevo at least thirty hours would have gone by. And Lucas was right. He would be too late to achieve anything. But he still had to go, he had to get close to Amra. And he would pray all the way that she was alive.

He went over the same chronology of events a hundred times. Lucas' call to Chloe had been at 6.30h, which meant about 13.30h in Nice. Krazicek had left Paris apparently several hours earlier so he could have arrived in Sarajevo any time that day. He himself was not going to get to Madrid until about 6.00h the following day, so as he landed, Krazicek would already have an eighteen hour head start. And Krazicek was a clever ruthless bastard who would run circles around the UN and local police.

But Nathalie would be in Sarajevo by then too. The unfaithful slut who had started this mess was probably his only hope. If she contacted Krazicek before he pulled the trigger there was a chance Amra might live. If he listened to her. And he had no idea if he would. Casual sex with one of doubtless hundreds of women in Krazicek's life would be unlikely to influence a man like him.

At this point his reasoning became circular and repetitive. Because he knew there was nothing Nathalie could realistically achieve.

And the fact that Amra was not picking up on her mobile was not easy to explain. She might have lost it or broken it. Go on clutching at straws George, they're all you've got.

ON THE WAY

AMRA WOKE UP with a smile on her face. It was 06.00h. This could be her last day in Bosnia. She'd spent so many years now trying to help her people, reason with the local politicians, influence and advise the U.N., travelling ..... She was not just tired, she felt the profound exhaustion of performing a hopeless and frustrating task.

She got out of bed, shook her beautiful head to clear her mind and splashed water on her face in the little en suite bathroom. Then she looked in the mirror. She hadn't looked so peaceful, her eyes so rested, for years. The power of clear thinking, of decisiveness. Clear your mind and your body responded. Much better than a workout in the gym.

She decided to go for a last walk round the town. It was still early. This would be her way of saying goodbye. She showered, washed her hair and changed into a tight pair of jeans and white blouse. She put on her sneakers and, unusually, some light make-up. She was not vain, she carried her beauty with modesty, even indifference.

But she took in her breath slightly when she saw her reflection in the long mirror. She added a touch of lipstick. Why was she feeling so coquettish? She suddenly realised she desperately needed to make love. And there was only one man she desired.

She walked out into the deserted streets towards the city's historical heart. Gazi Husrev-beg Mosque, Fehrat-pasha Mosque, the Orthodox Church of the Nativity, the Catholic Cathedral of the Heart of Jesus, and the Sephardic Synagogue were Sarajevo's main places of worship, all situated in the same area. They were so close in fact that it was as if they were huddled together for safety, even if the city seemed to have been taken over by Islam.

Croatians had returned to live in their homelands and the Serbs had settled in Srpska, in Pale (Radovan Karadzic's former stronghold), or in Banja Luka. The void left by their departure was filled by the arrival of Bosnian Muslim refugees, fleeing the country's Serbian and Croatian areas.

The new Islamic Sarajevo was visible in the lines of white Muslim graves on the hills that surrounded the capital and in the new mosques and madrassas built in the city, in the observance of Koranic rules and the number of women wearing the veil.

Sarajevo was now a city which evoked destruction and despair. Constant bombings, lack of food, water and electricity and being surrounded by Serbian forces in the 1990's had led to a violent isolation and a city landscape full of bullet holes and damaged buildings.

The single most important place Amra had visited upon arrival some eight years earlier was the Sarajevo Tunnel. This tunnel, which led to the airport (controlled by the UN during the siege of 1993-1995), had been the Sarajevans' only connection to the outside world and much-needed supplies. She would have liked to see it again, symbol of hope and ingenuity, but realized she didn't have time. The sudden need to leave was too strong.

She stared disconsolately at the rubbish everywhere. She wondered what it signified. Maybe people just didn't care any more. As she proceeded down the main thoroughfare touching the southern side of the market she glanced up at the mountains surrounding the town. Great for hosting the Winter Olympics in 1984. Great for snipers.

She was walking quickly, taking in everything, a sad adieu. She hopped on a tram that took her down to the park by the Vrelo Bosne river. It was clean there with cool waterfalls and shady trees. She went on to the Jewish cemetery, which was, apart from that of Prague, the biggest in Europe. Nobody really knew that. Her melancholy was further reinforced.

Finally, she spent ten contemplative minutes on the Latin Bridge where archduke Franz Ferdinand was assassinated, precipitating the First World War. She stood darkly on the exact spot where he was killed.

She had done her duty. She had said farewell to the city which once symbolized tolerance and multiculturalism, a bridge between Christianity and Islam. An entire culture had gone up in flames, just like the National Library, where almost all of the two million books and ancient manuscripts preserved there, Bosnia's entire cultural heritage, had been destroyed by a Serbian bomb.

She turned back resignedly to her hotel to tidy up, pack her belongings and set off in time for the meeting with Yerfdog De Vries. The man's parents must have been stupid or weird or both to choose a first name like that.

THE KILL

KRAZICEK ARRIVED IN SARAJEVO the evening before the kill. He checked into the Astra hotel on Zelenhi Beretki, a busy street in the centre of town. He casually noted the faded grandeur of the facade.

He found the suite of rooms to his liking. Dmitri had done a good job. Not only did the living room look exactly as he had instructed with two desks, each with a computer, but Dmitri had put a large map of Bosnia Herzegovina on the wall. There was also a telephone on each desk. It looked exactly like a provisional office.

Funny how maps always attracted one's attention. People liked to know where they were in their journey through life. He had no doubt that Amra would study the map, just as he was doing now. When she did that he would be observing her.

He went through to the bedroom and looked at the wall separating the two rooms. Perfect. He plugged in the electric drill he had brought with him and pierced a small hole. He looked through it and could see about a quarter of the living room. He moved across to the other side and drilled another hole. This gave a different perspective and revealed another quarter of the room.

Then he walked back to the living room and moved the two comfortable armchairs into the space visible from the first hole. He moved the map to the second visible space. She would either remain seated in one of the armchairs or, when she became restless, stand and walk to look at the map. He would pounce at the best moment.

He had decided to kill her with his bare hands. That picture he had in his mind of her slowly falling to the floor, looking with terror into his eyes as he crushed her windpipe, kept returning. Revenge would be sweet indeed, Vuk would be proud of him.

****

Nathalie, white with exhaustion and clutching her mobile, sat with Peter Dyson in a small UN office in the centre of town. It was already 09.00h and nobody had found or seen Amra. The police had been notified and had found her last address but she had moved out some weeks earlier. They were trawling through the hotels, both in Sarajevo and neighbouring towns.

Nathalie felt as if she'd been horse whipped. How could she still love that man? No, nothing could justify what he was going to do. Her brain started going numb and this relieved the pressure on her heart. She stared stupidly at her hands, beautiful hands which had caressed Krazicek's body with passion and love. And now she was helping to track him down. She twisted her fingers painfully and felt the cold sweat.

By 10.00h they had found the hotel where Amra had stayed but she had already checked out, half an hour earlier.

"So she's still alive, thank God for that," muttered Dyson.

She was alive at 9.30h thought Nathalie. Although she had been waiting desperately for news of Amra she didn't feel reassured. She knew Krazicek would be prowling close to her, like some enormous cat. Amra wouldn't stand a chance.

But if Amra wasn't dead already that meant that Krazicek could still get caught. He'd be locked up and she would never touch his body again. She forced herself to stop thinking before the confusion overpowered her.

****

Dmitri came to the hotel at 10.30h as instructed. The two men shook hands.

"You OK Dmitri?"

"Yeah. Do you like your new offices?"

"Perfect. This is what you have to do. Very simple. You wait here until she knocks at the door. You leave the door half open. You're really nice to her, give her a coffee and you say I'm late. My name is Yerfdog De Vries, never mind why. You smile, you make some small talk and after a couple of minutes you leave. The rest is my business."

"My pleasure Krazi. Anything for the girls eh ?"

"You got it."

Krazicek hesitated for a minute before he spoke again. He felt he had to share this. Dmitri was the only person.

"This isn't what you think Dmitri."

Dmitri looked at him with surprise. "I'm not sure I know what you mean Krazicek."

"The girl who's coming, Amra."

"What about her?"

"She's the one who killed Vuk. She's the fucking bitch who killed my brother!"

Dmitri's eyes widened and he said nothing for a moment. Vuk and Krazicek had changed his life forever. Nobody had ever bothered him since the incident at school, he had prospered despite the war and the word had got out that nobody could ever touch him because he was under their protection. He owed them everything.

"I will kill her?" he asked softly.

"I'm looking after that. I thought you should know. Just one detail. Can you fix the door so that when it closes you can't open it from the inside without the key?"

****

Amra got out of her taxi in front of the Astra hotel on Zelenhi Beretkia. The driver carried her two large suitcases to the reception desk and she paid and tipped him. He agreed to return and pick her and her luggage up at 13.00h and take her to the airport. She had decided to leave that very day.

She turned to the receptionist and asked for Mr De Vries' room number.

"Room 413, take the lift and it's is at the end of the corridor on your left."

The hotel was clean but shabby and the wooden panelling and red carpets gave it an old fashioned cosiness. Brave attempts at achieving an ambience, presumably Parisian, were evident in the imitation Louis X1V furniture and the black and white photographs of the Seine, the Eiffel tower and the Moulin Rouge.

Amra entered the lift.

SECOND DÉJÀ VU

THE DOOR TO ROOM 413 was ajar and Dmitri sat at one of the desks pretending to do some paperwork. The old fashioned television was showing the news. Amra approached with a flicker of interest and curiosity. This rendezvous was so appropriate somehow: a last attempt to help before she left forever.

She knocked gently on the door so as not to surprise the man at the desk and entered. The man looked up and registered pleasant friendliness on his face; and something else but she wasn't sure. All men looked at her in a certain way but this was different. More intense?

He came forward to shake her hand.

"Amra?" He asked with a smile.

"Yes. Yerfdog De Vries?"

A laugh. Slightly forced?

"Good lord no, I'm exactly the opposite. Yerfdog is one metre ninety five, he's enormous; I'm one metre sixty five. But we're good friends. We've known each other since childhood and this is our joint venture." Dmitri waved disparagingly at the makeshift office.

"'Save Bosnia'. It's a noble cause. I'm Bosnian, I can only thank you. Ask me any question you like."

"I'll get you some coffee first. Then I'm going to have to leave and Yerfdog will join you. He's the man to speak to, I'm more logistics and admin."

Dmitri went over to a table where a percolator stood with cheap white cups and saucers. He poured out the steaming black liquid carefully.

"Make yourself comfortable Amra, I'm going to have to disappear for an hour, so I'll leave you in the capable hands of Yerfdog, you'll really like him! Give him five minutes and he'll be here. Thank you again for coming, we really appreciate it. Catch up later OK?"

Amra nodded. She watched him leave the room and raise his hand in a small wave. Again, that strange look, as if he knew something about her. The door clicked shut. She sat back gracefully on the armchair and sipped her coffee. After a few minutes she glanced at her watch and felt a twinge of impatience. She started fiddling with her mobile, wondering whether to break her promise to herself not to turn it on for a week.

Krazicek watched her, his hatred and fury tinged with surprise. She was so beautiful. Maybe he would rape her. Sexy bitch. His eyes kept falling to her breasts and then her crutch. The trousers were tight. He started getting an erection and nearly laughed out loud at the perverted absurdity of the situation.

He watched her flip the mobile around in her hands.

Amra idly switched on the power and typed in her access code. As the screen lit up she pursed her lips slightly. There seemed to be a cascade of new messages, vocal and text. She sighed. It was going to be so good when she left this country. She stared at the ceiling for a minute and then clicked on the first text message.

Krazicek watched, frowning, as Amra read the first message. He saw her face go white and her mouth sag open. Strange, what was the bitch reading? What the fuck was the matter with her?

As he walked slowly into the room Amra did not look up. She just typed one word and pressed the send button. Then she closed her eyes. Krazicek knew something was wrong, but what?

"Good morning Amra."

She looked up at last, her eyes screwed into small slits, as if she was awaiting a blow. The message from Nathalie was only one minute old in her mind. She was still in a state of shock. No time to summon her strength. No time for anything except register, instantaneously, that this was where she was going to die. And Krazicek was going to be standing in front of her. She slowly opened her eyes wider. Vuk. She really was going to die.

"I said 'Good morning'." Krazicek approached slowly and slapped her so hard she felt herself lift off the chair and crash helplessly on the floor. She whimpered with the pain and the shock. A huge hand grabbed her hair and she felt herself lifted back. She was lost, barely conscious, caught up in a whirlwind.

"I've been looking forward to meeting you. The person who killed my brother. I hadn't imagined it would be a slut like you. A little Bosnian slut. I suppose you behaved like a whore and got him that way." He turned her over, undid her belt and pulled her jeans down.

Amra screamed only to feel the man's enormous hand close like a vice across her mouth. Krazicek ripped her panties off. Her eyes stared, terrified, at the floor.

Krazicek studied the smooth round buttocks; he pulled her belt off and tied her hands behind her with a rough piece of cord which he had brought with him. He whipped her once with the belt and then opened his fly. To his amazement he was too limp to penetrate her. Amra felt his flaccid prick vainly push at her sex. Her own hatred welled up as she squirmed in disgust.

"You're impotent," she screamed. "You're not a real man. Your brother would have done better however disgusting he was. If I hadn't killed him. He was a just an animal like you, a murderer....."

Krazicek roared with fury and started to beat her. She felt him punch her back, slap her buttocks, pull her neck back and spit on her face. He seemed to have lost all control. She felt her collarbone snap as he pulled her on her side and delivered another savage punch. Then she passed out for a few seconds.

Krazicek observed her. He fought back a tiny unfamiliar flicker of emotion. What the fuck was it? It made him feel uncomfortable. It made him refrain from delivering a final *coup de grace*.

The woman was so powerless in his mammoth hands she might just as well have been a child. In fact she looked like a child, such was her vulnerability and the strange innocence of her collapsed body.

The flicker of emotion was growing stronger. He hated it but could do nothing to fight it back. It was undermining his fury and hate.

When Amra came to, the beating had abated and she felt something wet on her back. Was it blood?

"Don't move a fucking inch. Bitch."

She froze. She couldn't believe her ears; she could hear suppressed sobs. The wet on her back? She wondered what to do. Better wait before she said anything more. She turned her head painfully so she could see him. He was leaning against the wall, his massive frame shaking and his right hand covered his eyes.

Krazicek felt something wilt inside him with every sob. What was the matter with him? He was shocked by his own attack, shocked by the sight of Amra's broken bloody nose, how she somehow kept her dignity despite her cramped inelegant position, half nude and covered in bruises and welts. Her left eye was horribly swollen and closed. She looked like a beautiful broken doll, savaged and torn.

"You shouldn't have said that," Krazicek whispered.

A heavy silence began to install itself. Amra began to feel more fully the pain which wracked her whole body. Was she going to die now? When would the sick giant decide to finish her off? Before she died she had to drink.

"Please, water."

Krazicek hesitated; but somehow it was normal. He felt the incongruous complicity between torturer and victim. God she looked bad. He'd done that to a woman? He started crying again as he went to the bathroom to fetch a glass of water. He splashed water on his face and held the towel to it until the tears subsided.

When he came back it was impossible to put the glass to her lips with roughness, she could barely tilt her head and, involuntarily, he gently caught the drops she couldn't swallow with his hand. He went back to the bathroom and returned with a wet towel. He tried to dab her eye but she groaned loudly and started crying in agony.

"I'm sorry," he said. "Something you said, the way you talked about my brother, the way you said you killed him.....it made me go mad."

Amra leaned forward an inch for another sip of water.

"Did you know he killed my entire family?" She whispered. "Except my brother. We were there, hiding. His men shot my parents and raped my sister. She was twelve years old. They left them dead, on the floor." She stared hopelessly at him.

Krazicek forced himself to look at the woman in front of him again. She had found her family dead and mutilated on the floor and Vuk was responsible? His twin brother .....

There was a pause. "And you don't like the way I talk about him?" Asked Amra.

Krazicek stood in silence.

Amra could still only whisper. "Because you are his twin brother you don't want to believe what you know is true. Everyone knows the truth about Vuk Racik. But mass murder is not the same on the page of a newspaper as it is when you see it happen in front of you. When it's your family. I would kill him, shoot him down like a mad dog, a million times and never regret it." It was Amra's turn to start sobbing uncontrollably.

Krazicek remained silent.

Then he sat by her and put his hand gently on her head, stroking her hair. He was no longer the man he had always pretended to be. He was no longer trying to please Vuk.

"I'm sorry. I'm so sorry."

****

Captain Harun knew all about Vuk Racik. Like most Bosnian Muslims. He had witnessed the war, lived through the siege of Sarajevo and lost his father and brothers in the Srebrenica massacre. He hated the Serbs in a visceral and unalterable way. He knew exactly who the real perpetrators were. He knew a lot about Vuk Racik. When he had heard about the latter's demise it was not without ambivalence. Yes, it was good that he was dead, but it was frustrating not to have pulled the trigger himself.

The UN alert that Vuk's twin brother was in Sarajevo and had to be tracked down before he murdered a Bosnian girl was astounding. Allah had given him a second chance to avenge the deaths of his father and brothers. Vuk Racik had been directly involved in Srebrenica and while no records could prove the involvement of Krazicek, nothing would dissuade Harun from joining the hunt. If Allah was kind to him he could be the one who exterminated him.

The UN had supplied the central police station with the name and number of Peter Dyson as their local liaison. Harun had sufficient personal authority to be able to take the initiative. He armed himself, ordered three of his best men to do the same, and set off with them to Dyson's UN offices on Zmaja od Bosne Street.

It was 11.45h when Nathalie's mobile signalled, with a small echoing ring, the arrival of a text message. It was half an hour after Harun's arrival. She fumbled, nearly dropped the phone on the floor and, with trembling fingers pressed on the message reception button. One word.

"What is it?" Asked Dyson.

"I don't understand, it just says 'Astra'. But it's from her, from Amra."

"Astra Hotel. That's where she is," said Dyson urgently.

"Stay here, I'll go with my men." Harun leaped to his feet and shouted orders at his subordinates. They clattered down the stairs and ran to the police car parked outside.

Nathalie stood up and spoke to Dyson. "I have to go there. You understand?"

Dyson nodded his head. "I'll drive you there."

****

Krazicek felt paralyzed by his own emotions and the impossibility of the situation. Amra had passed out again and the sight of her battered body made him hang his head in shame. He felt ashamed of himself for the sheer brutality he had unleashed on the woman. He felt ashamed to be the twin brother of the barbarous and manic man who had murdered her family. He felt ashamed of his own opportunistic and unscrupulous quest for wealth. He felt ashamed to be Krazicek Racik.

He felt ashamed of everything. A tidal wave of tearful repentance swept over him, his body started shaking again.

He wanted to put things right. Then he realized it was too late to put anything right except free the poor girl who lay in a pool of blood in front of him. Then he would disappear.

He knew exactly where to go. He had his bolthole in the Carribean, nobody would find him there. He would take Nathalie with him. She didn't have to know anything about what had happened. He would put together all his remaining resources, set up some kind of business and marry her. Be normal, have children.....

His hunting knife was strapped to his calf. Just like Vuk had always told him to do. He pulled it out of its sheath and stood over Amra grimly, holding the knife momentarily above her as tried to work out how to cut the tight cord without inflicting further harm on his victim.

As he bent to cut the cord which had already bitten into her wrists he felt a powerful blast of air accompanied by a deafening explosion. As he turned he saw the door of the room catapult off its hinges and crash to the floor almost at his feet.

Two men with assault rifles were kneeling on the floor in front of him, ready to shoot. A third man stood behind them, pointing his revolver at him. It happened quickly. Harun saw the knife, Amra's tortured body, and knew the same circumstances would never present themselves again. He could never be criticized for opening fire.

He pumped three bullets into Krazicek's torso and watched him widen his eyes in shock and then close them as he winced with the terrible pain. Krazicek slowly sank to his knees. Harun watched, his men stayed immobile. As the big man keeled over clutching his chest, Amra whispered something.

Harun stepped forward. "You're going to be OK. He will never touch you again."

"Don't kill him," she whispered.

"Don't kill him? Harun asked incredulously. "He was going to cut your throat." Very gently, he began to cut through the cord. He covered her with a blanket but didn't try to change her position. She seemed so broken that any movement might be dangerous.

The third of Harun's men walked through the door. He had held back to provide additional cover. The two others stood up, approached the writhing man on the floor and handcuffed him. Krazicek started changing colour, he was panting, totally helpless.

"How the mighty have fallen, huh Krazicek?" Harun looked at him with the sweet joy and exaltation of his revenge. The man was going to die soon. But he would suffer first.

He looked up. Peter Dyson entered the room with Nathalie. Shit, they shouldn't be there. Before he could object, Nathalie, who had taken in the whole scene in a few seconds, one hand covering her mouth, rushed forward to kneel beside her fatally wounded lover.

Krazicek could just whisper. "I wasn't going to kill her. I promise you. I was going to let her go."

Nathalie looked around in confusion and panic. "Help him," she screamed. She turned back and took his head in her hands.

"She drove me mad talking about Vuk. She drove me mad," Krazicek whispered, looking at Amra. "But then I understood. And now everything's too late; I'm dying Nathalie. Just tell me one thing. How come you are here, how did they know I would be here? How did this happen?"

He gestured with a painful nod of his head at Harun.

Nathalie wept bitterly, deeply.

"It's my fault," she said. "I knew you would be coming to kill Amra. You took the page from George's address book from my suitcase. I went back to Nice, to George's flat, got her number and texted her to warn her. The police were alerted, the UN was alerted......everybody was alerted."

The giant nodded his head again and blinked. The one woman he had loved in his life. This was his punishment. He would die in agony, betrayed by his lover.

"You did the only thing you could. There is nothing to forgive. I love you Nathalie. I'm sorry things have to end like this." He panted and winced again with the effort of trying to speak. His voice became a whisper. "Maybe Amra will forgive me. God, if he exists, will not."

Krazicek's body was spread-eagled on the floor, barely a metre from Amra's. Harun and his police officers were silent.

Amra gingerly stretched out a hand and touched his forehead. They stared at each other for a few seconds until the light went out of Krazicek's eyes.

Nathalie remained on her knees, Krazicek's head still cradled in her hands.

EPILOGUE

IT WASN'T REALLY ALL Nathalie's fault (I guess). Everybody has the right to be swept off their feet and that is basically what happened to the poor girl. So as I look back on things, I have forgiven her.

And much as I loathe Vuk Racik I have to admit that even though Krazicek was his twin he was not at all the same kettle of fish and it would be unfair to put him in the same category. Vuk was so terrifying you forgot that he was actually a very good looking (bastard) but Kazicek was more impressive than scary and he didn't have that maniacal look in his eyes. So he was even better looking. And, obviously, pretty irresistible to women in general and great company for men. If he wasn't dead I reckon I could even have become friends with him. How Krazi is that?

It was naive of Nathalie to go so far so quickly and the address book incident happened because she wouldn't listen to her conscience. But what if she had listened? I don't think it would have changed much. She had already given away Amra's name and probable location (before she knew Krazicek was Vuk's twin brother) so he would have tracked her down sooner or later. A man of Krazicek's intelligence and resources was more than capable of that. And if he had found her, in different circumstances that is, he might have killed her before he had time for his own conscience to get to work. He might have just shot her. But that's not the way it happened so Amra ended up alive and kicking, much to Nathalie's infinite relief and George's boundless joy.

There was something almost confessional about Krazicek's departure, that repentance, those tears of shame. I'm really not into any kind of religious "deal" as the Americans would say but the way Krazicek suddenly woke up to the fact that he was not Vuk "bis" and that he had his own integrity and capacity for decent feelings and emotions was, let's face it, a spiritual awakening to say the least. Unfortunately it happened just a few minutes before three bullets entered his massive chest.

It's weird, I feel really sad about his crossing the great divide. But before he did, I'm sure he must have felt a moment of expiation when Amra put her hand on his forehead.

Put it this way: Krazicek's sales of arms to Sadaam Hussein probably caused tens of thousands of deaths. But he didn't think about that, he didn't make a connection, he just focussed on earning vast sums of money because if he didn't do it then somebody else would seize the opportunity. Somewhere in his moral subconscious there was a blank page. So objectively speaking he was indeed one of the world's bastards but he wasn't psychopathic or sadistic or deliberately evil. A life sentence for what he'd done, yes, but not a death sentence. That's my take on it.

There is one sensational bit of news which I have to record now, I simply can't hold back any longer. Are you ready? Nathalie is pregnant! And, genes being genes, I suspect the baby boy (she's done an echography so she knows the sex) is going to be big. He'll probably measure about one metre ninety-five, be strong as an ox and captain the French national rugby team in about 2025!

So Nathalie is in a state of prenatal bliss and, tough little thing that she is, seems to have digested the Krazicek chapter without undue scarring. I talked to her a lot after Krazicek's demise and she just kept on saying "It would have been impossible anyway. I made my choice." I know what she meant. She chose to do everything possible for Amra to stay alive in exchange for the probable death of her lover. Tough choice.....tough chick!

George's "absence" which had insidiously been eating away at her relationship with him was of course his silent chagrin of love for Amra. Nathalie's infidelity (and here's the rather beautiful irony) actually led, via a long and dangerously sinuous path to George ending up with the woman he really loved.

Nathalie still lives on the Riviera, with a younger sister and, unbelievable as it may seem, has become part of the inner circle. The "famous five" has become the "famous six". I like her and admire her. We all do, especially Amra who feels indebted to her for the rest of her life. She's going to be a great mother.

By the way, in case there is some confusion about the sudden use of the first person singular, it's me, Lucas. George wrote the first book and I have written the second one. And, revenge being the driving force behind what happened over these few violent weeks I have described, the title of the book was irresistible.

Writing it has been fun, particularly as it hasn't needed any embellishments! What happened was already so unlikely and barely credible that adding anything more than what really took place would have been gratuitous.

I haven't told you about George yet. He was the most desperate to get to Amra, to save her, although he was the last person to find out she had survived.

He had switched on his mobile as soon as the Air Iberia flight touched down in Madrid. I had not let him down. I'd texted full details of a series of flights from Madrid to Heathrow and the connection to Sarajevo leaving at 10.30h. In six hours he could reach his destination.

He had stared at his mobile wondering what to do. There were no other messages. No news good news? He called me and I remember how destroyed he sounded. I did my best to distract him a bit.

"I'm getting my stuff together George, I'm coming back too. Chloe has been on the line and won't let me stay another day! Says she can't sleep without me, the children are out of control, people are beginning to ask where I am. My God, if they knew what we've been going through."

"What we *are* going through," he said.

"Yeah."

"So no news from your UN friends?"

"Sort of. I called the guy in Geneva and he said Amra hasn't been found and Krazicek remains totally invisible so as far as we know she's alive. But he said if they get a lead things could unwind very quickly because Sarajevo is so small. The police followed the lead Nathalie gave about him flying to Venice and they're filtering all the car hire companies. They're also stopping all cars with Italian plates in Sarajevo."

I could tell from George's silence that he had felt a tiny surge of hope which is what I wanted. Even if he was clutching at straws again.

Anyway, by the time his connecting flight eventually touched down in Sarajevo two ambulance teams had already arrived at the Hotel Astra. Krazicek's dead body was being transported to the hospital morgue and Amra, after a quick shot of morphine, to the accident and emergency ward. Captain Harun, accompanied by Peter Dyson and Nathalie, were following just behind.

I had been called by Dyson as soon as the ambulances left the hotel so when George fumbled for his mobile while his plane was still taxiing along the runway I'd had time to send him a text. I wish I'd seen his face when he opened it.

Amra alive, Krazicek dead! Told you not to worry like an old woman. Ask taxi to take you to "Kosovo" hospital, Traumatology Unit. Be prepared, she's beaten up but she'll survive. Bring her back to France, maybe it's time someone looked after her properly! Lucas

When he found Amra in the emergency unit of the "Kosovo" hospital he told me he didn't even mentally register her disfigurement. He didn't see the broken nose, the strapped shoulder, the swollen eyes, the bruises. He just saw Amra and started blubbing like an infant whose bottle has been snatched.

In fact he had a minor breakdown (amazing when you think about it, there was Amra, torn to pieces, saying "there there" to George who was, apart from his lachrymose condition, in perfect shape). He pledged his troth to the girl, at her bedside, and remained pretty much glued there for the next week while she gradually recovered.

When she did eventually emerge from intensive care, transiting through a normal ward for a few days, she soon regained her looks. In fact that new and barely discernible off centre twist to her nose made her even more sexy. I find it difficult to keep my eyes off her to tell you the truth!

And I'm so pleased for George, he's been transformed by the girl. He's lost that slighty killjoy side, that tendency to apply reason to situations which should not be....reasoned; you know, balking at that second bottle of wine at lunchtime, frowning at my excellent, albeit insalubrious, jokes, worrying about being late. He is now a joyful soul, the very incarnation of what the French call "insouciance". He lives with Amra in the centre of Nice and doubtless will waste little time in acquiring parenthood himself.

I don't have a great deal to say about myself apart from the fact I have the occasional nightmare about Vuk's reincarnation! I loved Costa Rica and yearn to go back although Chloe, perhaps understandably, is somewhat reticent about the idea. Does she sense that danger lurks in the unlimited diversity of the Costa Rican fauna? I suspect she does, because she has ended her love strike and seems bent on ensuring that her husband will not stray by giving him a very hot deal at home......which does make life simpler I have to admit.

So for the moment all is quiet on the southern front. How long will that last I wonder? I'm still on good form you know and I may just keep half an eye open for a bit of ......what exactly? I don't know. But I think you may be hearing from us again, particularly as I ponder Braden's proposition.

Before I finally put my pen down, I think I should tell you about our meeting with Braden. It took place about a month after George and Amra had returned, hand in hand, to Nice.

****

We arrived at CIA Headquarters in Langley at 8.00h as instructed. We were expected. At the main entrance we showed our passports, were given badges and pointed in the direction of Braden's office. It was a long walk, down multiple corridors and up in various lifts before we reached our destination.

Braden's office had its door open and he saw us as we hesitated at the entrance. He rose energetically to his feet, a broad smile on his face.

"Come in, please, great to meet you at last! Lucas? George?" He shook hands firmly and asked us to take a seat.

"This a quite a moment for me. Did you guys know you are famous in the CIA, particularly in the upper echelons?"

We looked at each other and shrugged our shoulders. We didn't know what to expect, apart from trouble. The British embassy (the ambassador no less) in Paris had advised us of our summons.

"Do we have a choice?" I had asked. According to the ambassador we did not.

We were scared but decided the only way was to go quietly, keep our dignity and maintain a facade of laconic indifference.

"Is that so?" I replied to Braden's question. I wished I had some chewing gum going. I was feeling really apprehensive and could only imagine that Braden's bonhomie was manipulative, that the mask would fall any minute. Softening us up no doubt, before the *coup de grace* announcing our imminent imprisonment and confiscation of assets.

"Yup," Braden had replied with an even broader smile. "You have achieved a lot."

George raised his eyebrows.

"Depends what you call achievement."

"Yeah, it sure does," Braden replied, looking more serious.

We looked at each other again. Shit, was this the moment when the cat stopped playing with the mice and got its claws out?

"Let me take you through what has happened. You guys knocked off Vuk Racik back in 1995. Correct?"

We both froze. He was going to go back that far?

"Is that correct?"

George thawed slightly and replied. "No."

"Hey, come on guys, I'm not here to accuse you or prosecute you about Vuk Racik. Shit, if I'd had the chance I would have sent him to hell with a bullet up his arse myself. I'm just summarizing things so we all agree on what you have managed to do over the last few years."

"The answer is still no," said George. "Someone else did it, someone with a good reason."

"So the money wouldn't have been a good enough reason?"

I broke in, still deadpan, trying to keep my pulse slow. "If you're not here to accuse or prosecute why so many questions?"

"Well it's all connected isn't it? Laundering Vuk's money, him getting killed and then you living graciously ever afterwards. What we didn't understand was how you were tempted to go after more. More than you needed. But that bit of greed opened up some interesting avenues for us to explore. The Teuber's were not even on our watch list until you went after them. Gerhardt certainly wasn't and Hans was way down the surveillance list. Then the transfers to Fairtrade took place and we traced back to your company, to Gerhardt Teuber and Hans Teuber and from there to your friend Pablo Jimenez. He went to see you Lucas, back in 1990. Long time ago."

I stirred uncomfortably. "I never did anything with Pablo Jimenez."

"No, not directly. But the introduction to Barantsteitbank in Liechtenstein came from you. Teuber had to note the source of business on the account opening form for the Panama company Jimenez was using. Mr Lucas Watt, manager Banque Helvas Nice. Made it sound very respectable."

"I had to send the bastard somewhere," I answered carefully. "I thought he was just a tax evader, I didn't know until afterwards that he was at the head of a Panamanian drug cartel. I told him I couldn't help but he was so fucking scary. I pointed him in the direction of Teuber. I thought it better to ingratiate myself with him."

"That's understandable I guess." replied Braden. "But you don't have to justify anything to me. You don't have to ingratiate yourself with me!"

That made me lose my cool. "I'm not trying to fucking ingratiate myself with you, or with anyone in your sick organization."

"Calm down, I was kidding. Anyway, Fairtrade came up on our flagging system thanks to you guys. Your transfer was big enough to attract attention. Then we saw three transfers to the same account, two of which originated from Costa Rica. We knew you were there. We put two and two together. The Fairtrade Ltd connection opened a Pandora's box. The account had been kept off the radar somehow by what we call the 'Sixth network' and some very hypocritical cover ups by the bank."

"UNSB?" Asked George.

"You got it. You see the 'Sixth network' was a network we knew existed, had to exist, given all the money flying around, but somehow remained invisible. We'd already unearthed five networks before this, all using the same sort of offshore structures and all leaving a trace somewhere. But the sixth one never left a trace."

"They must have done," I said.

"Yes and no," replied Braden. "We knew what they were doing, they were simply opening and closing offshore companies in multiple jurisdictions every time they did a transaction. The costs were minimal, maybe a few hundred bucks a company. So company A would transfer its balance to company B and get itself dissolved. Company B would form say five new companies in five jurisdictions and transfer on five amounts.

"Now imagine all the legitimate offshore companies being opened and closed and the sheer volume of transactions: trillions of dollars and billions of transfers in various currencies to hundreds of different banks in different countries. How do you sort the wheat from the chaff?"

"You don't," said George, "You just pray for a bit of luck, just one lead. And that lead was Fairtrade."

"Correct. And who gave us the lead?"

Neither of us replied.

"You guys are unbelievable. You're black swans........"

"What the fuck are black swans?" I Interrupted.

"Oh man, you haven't heard of black swans? They are the unexpected, freak or totally ignored elements or events which can shape history more than all the rational ones. Like why did adolescent street crime and gang warfare diminish in the late nineties? Because of President Clinton's social policies? No way. It's just that there were fewer homeless adolescents from single mother families wandering around looking for trouble because abortion was legalised in the seventies."

"OK, so what's legalized abortion got to do with me and George?"

Braden laughed. "You may be naive Lucas but not that naive."

"I always told you that you were a bit of a freak Lucas," said George. That made me smile; things seemed to be going in the right direction.

"I didn't say you were freaks," said Braden, "I just said you were freak elements, freak as in freak waves, freak as in......"

"I think we got the picture," I said.

Braden nodded.

"Fairtrade opened up a specific avenue of investigation, like I said. We traced back every movement on that account to when it was opened. Krazicek was a silly boy. He was so busy selling arms to Sadaam Hussein that he forgot to close Fairtrade and multiply his accounts. His relationship manager, a guy called Pelletier, opened up an even broader avenue, he was so shit scared by the investigation he traded in information on a pile of other dodgy accounts in return for a promise of a reduced sentence.

"So we checked the sources of his inwards transfers going back over three years. All of them emanated from offshore companies which no longer existed. But by going through the company registries in all the jurisdictions concerned we obviously found out who had formed them. Disreputable little corporate services providers dotted around the globe: Liechtenstein, Cyprus, Panama, Belize, Switzerland, you name it."

"Let me guess," I said. "You scared the living shit out of them and found out the names of the beneficial owners. I can just see your CIA guys swooping in, kicking down doors."

"Please Lucas." Braden looked genuinely pained. "Grant us some refinement. No, we did nothing for the first few months except monitor the company registries and note down and track every corporate entity formed by those DCSP's which we'd identified as being within the sixth network."

"DCSP's?"

"Disreputable corporate service providers," said George in a kind of condescending way which pissed me off.

I scowled at him.

"Then we applied a bit of pressure," continued Braden. "You are right Lucas, we scared them shitless, the DCSP's that is, and got all the names of the beneficial owners. Biggest scoop in the history of the CIA maybe. You have no idea of the numbers involved, it was like some kind of multiplier. A few million from an arms deal goes into one account, some BVI company for example, and then is dispersed across the world, like I explained.

"And then the same money is regrouped on some new company account, in Cyprus for the sake of argument, which when we investigate it turns out to belong to a drug trafficker. So the bastards making millions out of selling arms to Sadaam then reinvest the proceeds by buying drugs and their profits grow exponentially. And then guess what."

I shrugged, George looked from Braden to me.

"We found out, in this example, that the drug trafficker was using his profits to channel into Al Qaeda for Christ's sake!"

"So I guess you've been arresting a few suspects?"

"That is a beautiful example of British understatement. Yes, we've been filling a few prison cells and burying a few DCSP's. We've had three assassinations, not by us, we're not talking Robert Ludlum here, by the bad guys who were pissed off at having their identities disclosed. Oh, and as of today, we have five suicides."

I felt a bit overawed and posed the question I'd been posing myself ever since that telephone call from the British embassy.

"What the fuck is going to happen to us?"

Braden nodded. "Yeah, well that's what all of this is about. Think of who knows about your involvement in dismantling the sixth network: the Teubers, Charles Farrugia, and Krazicek Racik. Nobody else except us. Not even your wives or girlfriends."

"Krazicek is dead," said George, "so he can't tell anyone." Then he thought about Nathalie. Braden had failed to mention her. Good, she'd been through enough already.

"That's correct although it's a pity, for us guys in the CIA in charge of tracking him anyway. If he'd lived we would have had a greater direct insight into the whole 6th network and a lot of other stuff to do with Sadaam Hussein. He would have saved us a lot of work."

"The upper echelons of the CIA know about us too," I pointed out.

"Correct again. And you are our heros. We love you."

I found that ambiguous somehow.

"Does that mean you're not going to lock us up because you love us or you are going to lock us up despite the fact you love us?"

Braden just laughed.

"We wouldn't lock you up, all we're going to do is try and protect you. But we've thought about that too and the best protection for you would be for you both to go back to the French Riviera as if nothing had happened."

"What about the Teubers and Charles Farrugia?" George asked.

"Let's put it this way, the Teubers think you are little pussycats."

"What?"

"Yeah, you think you scared them?"

"Of course we did," said George. "Particularly Hans. He would never give us away."

"Crap," retorted Braden. "We pinned him down and he spewed out the whole story in a few minutes, all the details of all his 'special' clients, including Jimenez, and a full account of how you, Lucas, introduced him. He also told us how you kicked him around and blackmailed him."

"Fuck," I said.

"Don't worry, we told them you were working for us."

"Eh?"

"That's right. They believed us. They are both in prison right now."

Braden paused. Then he looked quizzically at us. "Ever seen a horny black man weighing twenty stone who wants to fuck you up the arse?"

George laughed nervously. "Er, not that often, why do you ask?"

"Well, they have. And they've been given to understand that this guy will be put in their cell with a triple dose of Viagra if they fail to forget everything that's happened."

"Why, why do all this to protect us?" I was grinning now.

"First we found out from Farrugia that you were going to put all the money into various kinds of charities and we liked that; secondly you guys have done a lot to bring down some of the most evil bastards in the world; finally the boss loves you."

"So we're free? Simple as that?" I asked incredulously.

"We're even going to send you $6.000.000."

Braden was looking amused. George leaned forward and looked at me. His mouth was open so I guess mine was too.

"What?"

"10% of USD60 million," he replied, "equals USD 6 million which equals exactly what you would have got in the first place if Krazicek hadn't intervened."

I sat back in my chair, trying to hide a smile of exaltation. Braden carried on talking.

"You guys were really stealing from the rich to give to the poor! How corny is that in the modern world? Robin fucking Hood, I love it."

There was one question remaining in my mind. "Listen Braden, this is all great but I've got to insist on one thing. Charles Farrugia. He had no idea about the background here. Don't put him in the DCSP category. I'd never forgive myself if he ended up in prison or committing suicide."

Braden nodded reassuringly. "Yeah, well, Farrugia was running scared until we made him a proposition."

Braden smiled engagingly at us. We were puzzled. And then I got it.

"Oh my God, you clever bastards."

"What's going on?" Asked George.

"Charles is going to go on forming offshore companies, particularly when he suspects foul play," I answered. "And when that happens he contacts our friend here."

"And he'll be well paid. Logically he's going to be earning a lot more than before. You guys are going to be pretty well off anyway but we'd like to have you on our side, you know, help us nail a few more of the bastards polluting this planet. Think about it. Someone in your position Lucas, bank manager with great contacts at H.O. level with the board of directors of Banque Helvas. Imagine the sort of information you could give us. And we can be pretty generous."

George was coughing. "He wants you to be a fucking mole Lucas. A mole working for the CIA. For Christ's sake…"

Braden stood up and apologised for not having a fridge with Champagne.

"This is CIA HQ, ain't no Private Bank that's for sure. Great to meet you and let me know if you want to help."

We just shook hands and nodded. Then we said goodbye and went for a drink. Several in fact.

Braden's last few words were echoing in my mind, echoing the very sentiments I had expressed to George at the outset of this, our second adventure.

'Nail the bastards'. Yes. It was like a revelation. I felt that surge of energy and lucidity, one of the best feelings in the world, the one you get when something is freed up inside you and you know where you really want to go, what you really want to do.

I suddenly became aware of George by my side, shaking my arm. I emerged from a sort of trance and realised I had momentarily cut off from him, my surroundings, the bustle around the bar, the laughter and the warmth.

"You OK Lucas?"

"Never felt better."

THE END

Printed in the United States
By Bookmasters